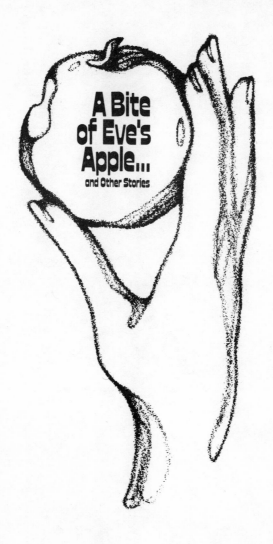

A Bite of Eve's Apple...

and Other Stories

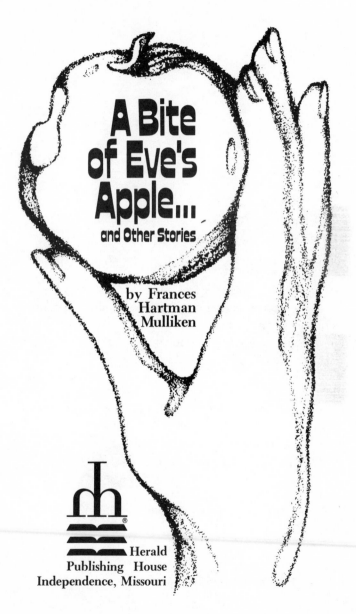

A Bite of Eve's Apple....

and Other Stories

by Frances
Hartman
Mulliken

Herald
Publishing House
Independence, Missouri

Library of Congress Cataloging in Publication Data

Mulliken, Frances Hartman, 1924-
   A bite of Eve's apple—and other stories.

   I. Title.
PS3563.U398B5   1983   813'.54   82-11757
ISBN 0-8309-0348-8

Printed in the United States of America

Contents

Preface

Many of these stories are based on real people and true situations. Names have been changed, of course, to protect the privacy of living persons. In most instances the places or circumstances have been altered also, but the facts are taken from life experiences I have witnessed.

These stories are about people, like you and me, who must decide each day what will be done with the intelligence, talents, and time given them. There is a commonality in our lives—the right of agency. Hardly a day goes by that we are not confronted with decisions. Our thought patterns become so instilled in us, and it is so ordinary to choose for ourselves that often we hardly think about the decisions we make, yet our everyday choices determine the courses of our lives. A wrong choice veers us off in a totally different direction than we would go if we took time to plan. We are, or may become, much the persons we want to be with this God-given agency of choice. With the choices we make, however, comes also the responsibility of our destiny both now and in the life to come.

It is not always easy to weed out human characteristics we all have, such as greed, selfishness, gossip, and the other negatives that can cloud our minds. It is not always easy to "turn the other cheek," "go the second mile," or "give the cloak and the coat also." But if we choose to serve humanity, to face each new day and mold into it something worthwhile and meaningful, the Holy Spirit is supportive of our efforts. Our days no longer slip by with opportunities and triumphs forever lost to us.

It seems a simple formula: plan ahead, and seek counsel if necessary. But those of us who have faced trials, problems, or situations seemingly beyond our control, know that the choices to be made are not always simple. We have to learn, painfully at times, to live life to the fullest, to accept joy and sorrow with equal grace, to give ourselves in service to the highest good in others and to ourselves, and to refuse to be satisfied with lesser life-styles.

To assist us on our way "toward the mark for the prize of the high calling of God" Apostle Paul gave helpful instructions in his letter to the Ephesians which have been preserved through centuries so that we in latter days may know how to persevere and succeed.

Every one of us is given grace according to the measure of the gift of Christ.

. . . Till we, in the unity of the faith, all come to the knowledge of the Son of God, . . . unto the measure of the stature of the fullness of Christ;

That we henceforth be no more children, tossed to and fro.

. . . Be made new in mind and spirit, and put on the new nature of God's creating, which shows itself in the just and devout life called for by the truth.

Then throw off falsehood; speak the truth to each other.

Can ye be angry, and not sin?

. . . If you used to be a thief you must not only give up stealing, but you must learn to make an honest living, so that you may be able to give to those in need.

Let no corrupt communication proceed out of your mouth, but that which is good to the use of edifying, that it may minister grace unto the hearers.

. . . Let all bitterness, and wrath, and anger, and clamor, and evil speaking, be put away from you. . . .

And be ye kind one to another, tender-hearted, forgiving one another, even as God for Christ's sake hath forgiven you.—Ephesians 4:7-32

Finally, it is not so much a matter of good versus evil, or even commitment versus indifference. It is a matter of self-respect, self-reliance, self-orientation, and self-discipline. In a recent *Herald* article, Elbert A. Dempsey, Jr., wrote "My hope is that we shall find our giftedness, acknowledge our sense of calling, and act in the example of Jesus. It will bring us the deepest satisfactions we can ever know, and only in this way can we bring to fruition God's purposes in us as a people."

To those who *try*, these stories are dedicated.

Frances Hartman Mulliken

Operation: Stewardship

The Christmas holidays lingered in Kathy's small suburban home like the aftermath of too rich food and too little laughter. Today, New Year's Eve morning, seemed a bit sour.

She sighed audibly as she stooped to pick up Bill Junior's dump truck, already scarred from a week's constant "dumping" since he first opened the long package under the Christmas tree. No telling how many nicks he had put in the furniture, and of course he had left the truck in the middle of the floor last night, even after she had told him specifically to put his things in his toy box. Surely a five-year-old boy was capable of having some responsibility!

A wail from the children's room announced two-year-old Carol's awakening. It was typical of Carol to greet the morning with the noise of a banshee. The wailing ceased as Kathy went into the room. Dark curls framed tear-filled brown eyes, and the sweetest pink-cheeked smile a child could give was offered to the mother/rescuer by her tiny replica.

Kathy sighed again. Of course she loved her children, but how time consuming they were! They kept her from accomplishing anything really important. The last

11

seven years of her life made her feel cheated somehow, as though she had just marked time since her marriage until she could get on with her own life. True, when she had met Bill Weston and had become his wife, she had married the dearest man on earth. She remembered how young and enthusiastic she had been in listing all his attributes to her parents and younger sister.

"Is Bill a member of the church?" her mother had asked.

"No—but he will be soon! He's so wonderful, he will certainly become a member within the first year of our marriage."

"Have you analyzed his faults as well as his good qualities?" Dad had asked with quiet concern. "Marriage is never to be taken lightly."

"Of course, dad. And he just doesn't have any serious faults. He reminds me of you."

Even her sister Eleanor had been hesitant to share Kathy's enthusiasm. "How can you marry a man who isn't handsome?" she had asked with teenage consternation.

"Bill does have big hands and feet; he's too tall; and his blond hair stands up at odd angles," Kathy remembered saying. "But those are the very things I love about him."

Kathy sighed once again as she tucked Carol into her high chair and started cooking cereal. She still loved Bill, but somehow she hadn't managed to tell him about the church during that first year together. Nor in the six years following had any change occurred in his straightforward, never-changing routine. Kathy had to admit that only his stability reminded her of her dad. And Bill did have a few faults which weren't improving with the years.

Throughout the day Kathy pondered over her status. Did others feel that time was running out, she wondered? At twenty-eight, just what had she accomplished? Were the love of her family and the respect and friendship of her neighbors not enough to satisfy her? What was lacking to make her life complete?

By five o'clock she was truly frustrated. She would never be fit to go with Bill to their neighbor's to see in the New Year. Her Saturday work was still not entirely finished. Carol was taking such a long nap she would be difficult to get to bed tonight before the sitter arrived, and Bill Junior with the aid of his new dump truck was transferring pebbles from the driveway onto the long winding walk. Tears began to roll down Kathy's cheeks, and she didn't try to check them. Nerves, she thought. Perhaps a good cry is what I need.

"Mommy," yelled Bill Junior, "May I go over to Davey's to play for a while?"

Kathy sniffed and dabbed her eyes. "No, dear. Daddy will be home soon, and you need to take your bath before dinner."

"Mommy, why are you crying?" Bill Junior's eyes were wide and serious. "Don't you love us?"

"Of course I love you. I just have a headache. Why on earth would you feel I don't love you?"

Bill Junior crawled up on her lap and put his arms around her neck. "I thought you maybe didn't love us because you're so cross all the time."

Kathy was shocked. Were her feelings so apparent a five-year-old could detect her unhappiness? If so, what did Bill think?

13

"I'm sorry, dear," Kathy stammered. "I'll try not to be cross any more."

The boy snuggled closer, basking in the assurance that all was well with his world. "My Sunday school teacher says that when we feel mean or unhappy Jesus will help us," he offered.

Kathy kissed the top of his unruly blond hair, so like his daddy's. "You know something? I think he has already helped us."

How long has it been since I went to church school? Kathy wondered. Or, for that matter, when did I last attend a church service? It was so hard even to have the desire to go without Bill, and he had never seemed interested in going with her. Then, too, it was about all she could manage on Sunday morning to get Bill Junior off to his class without the extra work of getting Carol and herself ready.

Kathy gave her son a hug as she playfully pushed him off her lap and headed toward the kitchen to start preparations for the evening meal. She caught a glimpse of herself in the hall mirror—a ruffled Christmas apron over faded denims and a smile fleetingly brightening her face. Were there two personalities in her—one happy, one cross—vying with each other?

Perhaps religious activity was the answer to the unrest she had felt gnawing within her. If her son's simple suggestion could help solve the problem it might be that she, in turn, could have a closer comradeship with Bill. She would have to work alone for a little while, but perseverance would surely get results, just as it had in the preschool dad's group Bill headed now, and the Chamber of Commerce board job she had talked him into taking. Knowing that she was truly interested in an objective had often caused Bill to consider it too. How foolish she had been, Kathy decided, as she shoved golden corn sticks into the oven. She had concealed her religious convictions from the person who meant most to her in life. True, Bill might never find his place in the church, but she could not know unless she gave him the opportunity. And their children would become members with training. There would be no hidden loyalties between them ever again.

Kathy paused a moment while setting the table to breathe a prayer of thankfulness that she could at last understand herself and the need within her. Out of the mouth of babes. . .thank God for the truthfulness revealed by her small son.

What greater purpose could life offer than the sharing of the gospel with her loved ones? And tomorrow, Sunday, was New Year's Day. . .a reason for making a fresh start—if indeed she needed one.

Challenging her was a tremendous stewardship, and Kathy was satisfied to look and work toward its fulfillment.

Life
in a
Straight
Line

Outside the trailer an early morning sun shone warm on the palms. A mockingbird called somewhere close to the trailer, and an answer came back like an echo farther along the line of mobile homes.

Betty Dunbar, pulling on her hose, neither saw nor heard the miracles of nature. She had disliked Texas from the first moment they had arrived, and she had no intention to start searching out its beauty now. She dressed hurriedly, glancing now and again at her husband, still sleeping.

Finished except for a few last-minute preparations, she walked softly down the narrow hall, past the bath and the extra bedroom they used as a library, to the kitchen. She thought about Bob while she prepared breakfast. He would be all right without her for a week or two while she went north for a visit with their son and his wife and the new baby. They had called and asked her to come to help, and Betty was glad to be needed. More than this, she knew that she was secretly delighted to get away from cramped quarters into a real home again. . . *her* home.

She looked past the tiny kitchen table into the dining

16

room, and beyond into the living room. The trailer was nice. In fact, it was the best money could buy. It was just such a letdown after years of having her own home and being "in control" for Bob's sake. Now the home belonged to Leslie, their son's wife, who would love it for Steve's sake.

Betty thought about Leslie, about her contemporary ways. She seemed so incapable of caring for a new baby. Perhaps she and Steve should have waited another two or three years to start a family...although she was nearly six years older than Betty had been when she married Bob. Girls these days, however, didn't seem to know much about home, family, housekeeping—and cleaning silver.

"So, you're up and ready to go. Wouldn't be anxious, would you?" Bob spoke from the doorway, tying his robe around his pajamas. Except for his graying hair he looked as young and well as he ever had.

"Guess I am a little eager," Betty admitted. "Are you sure you won't go with me?"

"No." He was firm. "I'll wait until the little fellow is old enough to know that a granddad is good company. And I want none of that midwinter snow."

Betty put juice and toast on what seemed to her a miniature table. She bumped her knee as she sat down. "Do remember to take your medicine," was all she allowed herself to say, grimacing as she rubbed her knee.

After breakfast there was a rush to get ready to go to the airport. Bob put her luggage in the car and stood waiting on their patio, surrounded by the tropical blooms he kept in pots and window boxes. Betty glanced once more around the rooms, working her way along the straight line which was now their home, making sure all was in order. Since Bob's heart attack two years ago they had lived in a trailer, and she guessed that was to be her unpleasant lot the rest of their lives. With a sigh of relief she left it behind her.

Outdoors she did not feel the coolness of the shaded patio or the breeze off the ocean. She felt only her elation at leaving this village of impersonal rectangles, lined up row after row. They were like dominoes. If one were to topple, they would all fall down. Then, because she loved Bob—and it had been his illness which had brought them here—she smiled at him and said, "I'll miss you, sweetheart. Call me every night."

He looked at her in his special way, and she was content for the moment. I've fooled him, she thought. He doesn't suspect for a minute how much I hate life in a trailer.

All the way to Chicago Betty reminisced about the old days in her lovely home overlooking Lake Michigan. They had been so happy together with their fourteen rooms, spacious porches, two patios, and seven acres of trees and shrubs and gardens.

Their son Steve had taken the home, of course, and now he and Leslie would rear their son here just as Bob and she had reared him. Baby Bob would have a pleasant life. She hoped there would be another child three or four years along the way so her grandson would not be as lonely in the large house as Steve had been.

Steve met her at the airport, and it took another two hours on the toll roads to reach home. Betty felt she was truly coming home, and a tingle of anticipation kept her fidgeting. Steve's driving was like his personality—relaxed, unhurried.

As they approached the house the white brick exterior

looked the same as ever, curving graciously with the land, overlooking the lake.

"My, that wind off the lake is cold," Betty said as she followed Steve into the house. "The wind chill index must be far below zero."

"I can see you're a southern lady now," her son joked. "The nippy air has moved on: This is a warm period we're having."

Betty shivered and closed the door behind them before Steve could put down her luggage.

Indoors the home was as beautiful as she remembered it to be, though some changes became evident as she glanced about.

"You see we've livened up the old place a bit," Steve was saying.

"Yes, I see you've had some painting done." Betty looked long at the cream-colored paint covering the cherry woodwork she had loved so much. The painted wood was attractive, but the elegance was gone. Her pale greens and golds were now apricot and sage.

"We've done most of it ourselves," Steve explained. "It's hard to get workers these days, and besides we live on a budget. Most painters and carpenters contract for subdivisions and apartment buildings—more money for them if there is volume."

"Welcome home, mother," Leslie called as she bounced down the winding steps from the second floor.

Betty's first impulse was to stop her from coming down the steps so fast, but Leslie looked radiant.

"Yes, it does seem a lot like coming home," she said, while her mind wondered at this girl who gave birth, regained her figure within two weeks, and bounded around exuding love and health. When Steve was born

19

she hadn't even gotten out of bed for several weeks for more than an hour or two at a time.

"Little Bobby is asleep now, but he'll sure want you to hold him after you've rested and he wakes up."

"You let people hold him?"

"Of course, He's a person! In the meantime, we could stand a warm drink," Steve spoke up.

"It's already perking. You'll love it, Mother," Leslie said. "We found this great beverage made from grain—no chemicals, no caffeine."

Betty didn't know where the time went. A month was gone before she knew it; there was so much to be done. She had forgotten how big the house was. Leslie had a day-lady come in once a week (she said she would rather do her own work, but she would accept help for another month or two) yet she could use assistance in getting organized. She had lived in an apartment before her marriage.

Betty made out a daily routine which helped bring order out of happy chaos. Nothing seemed to bother Leslie. . . that was the whole problem, as Betty saw it.

By the end of six weeks all began to run smoothly except for those times when Bobby disrupted the household. It seemed that Leslie and Steve were going to allow it. The baby had them on a schedule instead of the other way around, and neither gave any indication of minding it.

Betty did not remember the old nursery (now changed from pale yellow to red, white, and blue) being so large. It seemed like wasted space, and she suggested that a divider would turn the large room into both bedroom and play room as Bobby grew bigger.

"Good idea, mother," Steve said. "We can do it to

several of these big bedrooms as our family grows."

"More projects for us to work on," Leslie added delightedly.

"Well, I was thinking you might want one more child to grow up with little Bobby." Betty blushed slightly, thinking she shouldn't talk about their plans and their intimate affairs.

"*One* more! We want a whole house full." Leslie giggled at the thought.

"There's a lot of talk about population explosion," Steve said, "but we feel it isn't a matter of number; inadequacy is the real problem. With this big house and seven acres, we figure there is plenty of room to teach independence and self-reliance. We can have a little Zion right here. And if we don't have our own children, there are always others needing homes."

Betty didn't say anything, because she frankly did not know what to say. It made her tired to think of all the work involved in rearing a large family. Both Leslie and Steve seemed so relaxed about everything, maybe they would pass this on to their children. *Maybe* there wouldn't be problems and personality conflicts and adjustments. . . but she knew better. That was all part of life.

Betty plodded on through several more days. There was just not enough time to do all the work she had once done so easily with the help she had hired. Though she had always loved *objects d'art*, she was glad Leslie's taste ran to simpler decor. It eliminated a lot of dusting. After cleaning four and a half baths one morning when the day-lady called to say she was skipping that week, Betty thought it was a bit unnecessary to use all of them and said so. When four hours were required to wash and

21

wax the kitchen, pantry, and family room floors, she hinted that indoor-outdoor carpeting might be warmer for the baby when he started crawling.

The week Betty decided to go back to Florida the snow began in earnest. At first it was fun, seeing the feathery flakes come down, covering the grayness of the last snow. Three or four inches had not been much to contend with, but now it was building up and up. After three days it didn't seem so wonderful.

"Don't you have someone to do your snow shoveling for you, Steve? If this gets much deeper you won't be able to get in or out of the drive."

"Oh, sure," Steve reassured her. "The man who does the yard work has a snow plow. He'll do it when he gets around to it. If he doesn't have time his kids will do it, but I always tell him to be sure the church walks and parking lot are done first."

"When he gets around to it? When his children get around to it?"

"That's the way it is these days, mother. I'm just lucky I can depend on him to get here sometime after the snow stops. I'm thinking of getting a small snow plow myself, for in-between times when we need it."

Betty decided to shovel the walks herself. She knew it was a protest of the changes since her days here, and at first the strain of muscles exhilerated her. The snow was heavy, and the cold wind off the lake howled at her until it drove her back indoors.

*   *   *

"It's impossible to say how much you've helped me," Leslie told her mother-in-law.

"I'm happy for that," Betty answered, folding dresses

22

to fit the luggage. "Believe me, you've helped me a lot too."

On the plane Betty thought with pleasure of the beautiful home which had been hers, and of the lovely young family—her family—now enjoying all the things she and Bob once had loved. She thought of the brick walls, secure and strong, the wonderful corners of the house, jutting out into the wooded landscape, the curves of the stairs, and the bay windows. It pleased her to think of it, and to remember the good life they had shared there when they were younger. She thought for the first time since Bob's illness that she was glad to be leaving it in younger, more able hands. She was truly grateful, too, that they had been able to educate their son so that he would have the money to keep the house, the grounds, and the children who would need his help.

Bob was waiting as she left the plane. He looked tanned and relaxed and rested. It was obvious he had gotten on very well without her!

"It's a good thing I came home. You'd never remember to get a haircut without me to remind you."

"I did remember. Three times in two months, as I usually do, and that's on schedule with this thick hair of mine. I'm letting the sideburns grow out again a little."

"Oh...that's why you look different. Well, I'll just have to get used to it."

"How was everything?" Bob asked as he drove. He said it slowly, as though a lot depended on her answer, and his knuckles were white on the steering wheel.

"Time enough to tell you all the news over dinner, and later tonight, and probably on into tomorrow. I'm eager now just to get home."

He looked at her, but she was leaning close to the

window. From the highway Betty could see the long rows of trailers interspersed with palms and flower gardens. Only the patios and the flowers and the colors of the trailers made them individual. But somehow they looked clean and trim and very, very sensible for an aging couple with one heart attack on the debit side of their ledger.

"I just can't tell you how great it is to be back with you." She gave him a pat, then looked again at the trailers. They weren't dominoes anymore. They were solid bricks in a garden wall, and they would never all fall down. She looked on both sides as Bob turned the car into the long drive. These were no longer trailers. . . they were *homes*. Mr. and Mrs. Carpenter lived here, Greg and Patsy Fitzpatrick lived over there. Mr. Terry had painted his trim canary yellow. A new couple had moved in; she must make them feel welcome in the neighborhood.

Bob grinned at her as he pulled into their car port. "You look as if you're seeing this place for the first time."

"I guess I am." Betty answered. "And I like what I see."

She realized suddenly that lack of complaint had not fooled him much about her feelings. "I've learned something, Bob—something very important. There is only so much living we can do, no matter where we are, no matter how large or small the place we call home. The only thing that really matters is what we do in that living space. . .how we reach out and help others. . . and recognize the blessing that we are living it together."

God
So Loved
the World

Martha Drewsner paused momentarily in the last block to look at Sheila McHugh's early tulips. They were arranged in neat circular beds surrounded by washed rocks, and the array of varied colors was beautiful after the long, cold winter. She might well stop to enjoy the flowers, but they alone were not Martha's reason for stopping now. The four blocks from her home to the church seemed longer each year, and this morning particularly she needed the excuse of admiring the tulips so she could catch her breath.

The horn of a passing car was honked twice, and she looked up in time to see Lila and Brent Kinney wave to her. A half block farther on Lila's two children waited with illustrated church school lessons to show their parents between church school and the Easter worship service.

My, how those children have grown, Martha thought as she started again toward the church. They were just little ones when their daddy died. Let's see. . . that was ten years ago this spring. Lila lost her Charles the same week I lost my Ted. Such tragedies. . . such waste of life!

The steps were steep, and Martha was puffing a bit as she went into the church foyer, resting briefly to calm her rapid heartbeat. Lila was smiling up at Brent; he had a supporting arm across her back as they stood to one side of the large double doors leading into the sanctuary.

Martha began to fan herself with her bulletin to take some of the flush from her cheeks.

Lila is happy with Brent, she thought. The scar of her loss has healed, and she has found happiness again—even a good father to share his love with her children, but my son can never be replaced. He left no wife or child for me to love.

In the innermost part of her, bitterness broke out anew to surge through her body. Martha continually fought against the bitterness, in fact she thought she had conquered it, but here it was again—going through her in hot waves that almost nauseated her.

The midservice announcements were ended, and persons waiting in the foyer began to move into the church. She felt someone touch her arm and looked up to see the Kinneys smiling at her.

"We'll pick you up next Sunday," Brent said. "Lila mentioned this morning that there is no point in your walking when we come right by your home."

"Why, thank you, but that really isn't necessary. . . ."

"Of course not, but we would enjoy having you ride with us," Lila interposed. "I always take the children to church school, then pick up Brent for church. He works nights, but he can make it in time for the worship service."

"Wait for us after church and we'll take you home," Brent said.

Martha was ushered into a pew near the front. She liked being seated near the rostrum because she could

hear the organ, the prayers, and the minister. Strange
how age pushed a person past the back rows where the
teenagers sat and whispered and wrote notes, past the
young mothers and fathers seated close to the door to take
out noisy children, past the middle-aged church workers
who were anxiously engaged in giving their reasonable
service in time, money, and experience. Strange, too,
how ready a person could be for the front seats where
there would be no distractions from the service except
one's own thoughts.

"'Create in me a clean heart, O God; and renew a
right spirit within me,'" Martha prayed. "Forgive the
bitterness which welled up within me when I envied the
happiness of those who had kindness and good intent
toward me. And, Father, I pray once again for the peace
and understanding I know one day will be mine when I
have learned to accept fully the death of my only son!"

The choir was singing, and Martha ceased her prayer
to listen to the promise of resurrection.

> *Alleluia, Christ is risen,*
> *Alleluia, Christ is King;*
> *Death is vanquished,*
> *Life's eternal,*
> *Let all men with gladness sing.*

For ten years Martha had listened to the Easter
anthems with a heavy heart but always with the hope
that here she might find the answer she sought. This
year Easter was no exception.

Her husband had died before their son Ted was old
enough to walk. I will be both mother and father to him,
she had thought. I will protect him and teach him the
valor of manhood. Rearing her son had become her
whole life.

Ted had joined the army to prepare for a career. This had provided schooling Martha could not have afforded for him. He was a fine young man with a good position as a helicopter pilot. Then, on a sunny winter day in Martha's town, she awakened with the coldness of fear covering her—a fear of something she could not name. One month later the country was involved in a war few people had expected. Through two years Martha had continued to live in the fear that had encased her since that morning she had awakened with the taste of it on her lips. Just a few months before the war ended she had received official notice of Ted's death. The day had been warm and sweet with the scent of flowers in the air, but Martha had died too, that day, in her heart. The fear had finally won.

"He was brave and courageous," a chaplain had written. "You will be proud to know that he died as a result of action beyond the call of duty; it was his quick thinking and self-sacrifice which saved at least eight other men. Had he not volunteered to scout the area one more time in the helicopter they would not have been reached. No one knew until he brought them in that he had been wounded."

The choir had finished the anthems and the pastor was reading the scripture text: "For God so loved the world, that he gave his Only Begotten Son, that whosoever believeth on him should not perish; but have everlasting life."

"*His Only Begotten Son.*" Martha's mind clutched at the words. She had read them probably a hundred times. . .but had she *really* read them? It had never before occurred to her that God had given his *only* Son to overcome the wickedness of the world. Of course the words were familiar to her, but somehow today they held a new meaning. This was something she could understand because of the similarity of her experience in having given her only son to a war-torn world.

In my selfishness I have considered only my loss, she thought. Surely there are parents the world over who have experienced the same feelings I have. Our heavenly Father knew the bitterness of an only son's death, yet he gave him because of his love for all creation. Martha's eyes filled with tears at the realization, and she lifted her face to see the morning sunshine reflected on the Easter lilies flanking the altar.

The pastor paused. Then in the hushed tones of conviction he continued, "Christ truly died that we might live. He sacrificed his own life that all other persons could have life more abundantly."

Martha felt the beginnings of understanding at last: death is not important—only life, how one lives and for what purpose one's life is spent.

The knowledge that Ted, too, had given his life for others consoled Martha. He had followed the great example of his Savior. Ted had loved the world and believed that somehow military service to his country would help make it a better place to live.

The sermon had ended when Martha again brought her attention to her surroundings. At last she was filled with the spirit of peace, and it was radiated in her eyes.

When she walked out into the noon light Martha saw the Kinneys waiting for her. As she hurried to meet them the words of the anthem reechoed in her heart:

> *Death is vanquished,*
> *Life's eternal,*
> *Let all men with gladness sing.*

Masterpieces

My family is in favor of my attending our local art club. My husband encourages me to exhibit my own paintings, and I'm sure he is proud to slyly remind his friends that his wife studied art in Paris two years before we were married—this, of course, when I win a ribbon or monetary reward for a particular hanging. My children speak their praise more openly, volunteering me for everything they consider "artistic." No one in the family, however, is in favor of disrupting his or her schedule for my art club meeting on Saturday.

Today I hurried through lunch with the children and took Jody to the library for the afternoon. She is our studious one, and—I hope—a future Graceland student. After the trip to the library I drove across town to pick up a baby-sitter for our other two, Jeff and Patty, who always seem highly insulted that they have a sitter. I hurried back home and left Mrs. Myers, along with instructions to the children on how to treat and how *not* to treat her while I was away. I left, hoping their father would return early from his golf session.

I felt a little guilty as I drove to the club. Basically a mother should be able to ask her children to do something and, without attaching stipulations and bribery, expect it to be done. Something would have to be done about this, and I made a mental note to be more understanding, or more strict, or whatever it might take to gain the confidence of my two young ruffians, so they would learn accountability.

By the time I reached the clubhouse, parked the car, and hustled up the steps, it was as I had expected. The business session had already begun. This, of course, would be followed by a program of some undetermined merit, which would then be followed by the art exhibit itself. Polly Ashby, club president, would be furious with me for being late. It was so easy for Polly to be places on time that she could not find any leniency for tardiness in others. I decided an inconspicuous entrance might be best—between business and program.

As I moved closer to the club room I noticed that another occupied the lounge as well as I. It was a man, sitting alone by a window, looking aloof and reflective. He must be the speaker. As I watched him he became aware of me and flashed a smile of recognition. I did not know him, I thought, yet he definitely looked familiar. Somewhere I must have seen a photograph of him.

He arose and walked toward me. "Ah, it is most wonderful to see you again, Mademoiselle. Or is it Madame now?"

"Do you mean me?"

"But, of course. Are you not Mademoiselle Virginia Cook, who studied art in Paris some years ago?"

"Monsieur Du Bon," I gasped. His hair was white now, and his face thinner—with intricate fine lines at the corners of his eyes and mouth.

— — —

The years rolled away, and I stood young and fresh on the roof of the Hotel de la Place. I had noticed the man before. He had often been leaving the apartment hotel as I entered. A number of times he had taken the self-service elevator as far as the fourth floor when I was going up to my own rooms on the eighth. Usually the small elevators in Paris were not shared by unknown persons, but the hotel management encouraged friendliness among student patrons.

The man had never been on the roof before in mid-morning. Few of the tenants took advantage of the scattered chairs until late evening when they could look down on the city lights and feel the night breezes. Then there was laughing and drinking of wine, and families and friends grouped together. I was not a part of that life, so I avoided it.

Ordinarily at this early hour the roof retreat was as solitary as one's private apartment, without telephone or service interruptions. This is why I ventured up there. I had made one trip already, to take portable easel and oils. Now I carried brushes, turp, and palette.

"How do you like Paris, Mademoiselle?" he asked, turning to see my canvas.

"Very well." My answer was curt. I adored Paris, but I felt it was my own affair.

"Very good view from here for your painting, *oui?*" He continued, quite undaunted by my coolness. "Also you use other mediums than oil? You perhaps paint with watercolors? Pastel?"

I was aware of his apparent knowledge of paints, but I refused to let this disarm me. He was a stranger, and though he had every right to be on the roof at this time of morning, I felt he had invaded my private sanctuary.

"I have used other mediums, such as charcoal," I replied with as much ice in my voice as I could muster. "I prefer oils."

"Ah, yes. It is understandable, because your style indicates the preference. But it is good to use all until techniques are thoroughly developed."

This man was no different from others whom I had met—friendly, interested in an American. He was being courteous in keeping his conversation on my obvious interests. I simply did not wish to talk with him.

The man was smiling now. He sensed my reluctance to talk, of course, and it amused him. "Everyone here is friendly, anxious to be of help to the student from America," he said. "You dislike so much being disturbed as you work?"

"No, it isn't that," I answered falteringly, my ice melting in spite of my resolve. I knew it must be the unknown customs and the intense interest in foreigners the French displayed which disconcerted me. "I had not expected anyone to be here this morning, that's all. And my French is so limited."

I had finished lamely, especially since the man had spoken in English. He nodded, seemingly not noticing my words. He stepped closer to the canvas, backed away, and then walked slowly toward the easel again.

Had he not said then what he thought I might have gone on about my work that day without ever thinking of the man who turned to look at it. It was a chance meeting, it seemed, but it stayed in the back of my mind a long while, until marriage and children and the press of activities in a young matron's life in America had crowded it out. Now, facing this same man, I had met casually on a rooftop in Paris, I recalled each detail of that meeting. I remembered the conversation, the advice, the predictions he had made.

"You are a lazy artist," he accused, looking at the study of colors and shapes I had reproduced. "You are painting only what you can see."

I had not asked for his opinion. I did not know him, had no interest in his opinions, and disliked his comments concerning my labors. I set about getting my oils ready for further work without replying.

"So, I offend you because I speak frankly," he went on. "Or perhaps because I speak the truth? I am sorry, Mademoiselle. But one with such talent should put it to work, *oui*? You work, but you do not set your paints to working for you. You do not give them a life of their own to flow and create and imagine."

"I haven't the faintest idea what you are talking about, Monsieur," I answered, as I splashed oils and turpentine and indiscriminately dipped brushes into the mixtures.

"Ah, but you do. That is why you are angry."

Of course I knew what he meant. I might as well be painting a scene from a postcard as spending my attention on the actual scene before me. There was no atmosphere in my painting, no vivacity. No one would be able to look at my street scenes and hear the honking of horns, the laughter of people sitting in a sidewalk cafe, the faraway beep-beep of a police patrol wagon. No one would be able to smell the myriad smells of Paris or see the bursting of spring buds. The throaty coos of pigeons in the square before the opera house and the prayer bells on the Church of the Madeleine could not be heard in my paintings. Odors of baking pastry and the pungent aroma of wine were lost when I tried to record them.

"I am a student at the Technological School of Arts," I quipped. It was the only parley I could think of at the moment.

"I know. You are Mademoiselle Virginia Cook. Your instructor has great hope for you, for you have true talent lying just below the surface of your work. Few artists have talent, you know. This is true. They have other attributes. . . a passion for painting, a sense of design or of color, or sheer determination. . . but not true talent. That is why it is so important for you, a gifted one, to use yours well."

I stopped painting and looked at the man. He was perhaps forty, with a sprinkling of gray about his temples. Dark-complexioned, he might have been a native of any of the southern European countries, yet I sensed he was French. He was friendly; he was inquisitive; he was quite sincere. And he had hit exactly on the theme dearest to my heart: a gift, a talent must be used, not buried. That's why I was here; it was a part of my religion, a part of my giving of myself to the glorification of God. The fact that he knew so much about me did not at the moment alarm me but rather added emphasis to his critique.

"Are you an art instructor? I asked.

"No. I am a gifted artist."

The simplicity of the statement was quite typical of his nationality.

"I do not yet consider myself an artist," I said at length. Somehow it seemed pushy to me to acclaim one's self.

"No. . . you are not," he agreed slowly. "But the truth

35

is that you well could be an artist if you had the determination."

"Well, it is something at least to be told one has the capacity." I was more than a little annoyed at this intrusion of my time and I wanted to be rid of this self-appointed analyst of my abilities.

"You are a lazy artist," he repeated. "You do not set your paints working for you."

"I know," I answered sarcastically. "I need to lock myself up in a room and see no one until I have created the masterpiece of my soul. Maybe I should sketch the dancers at the Lido, or become the mistress of a nobleman." I had said more than I had intended, and my face burned with embarrassment.

The man had not laughed at me. Nor had he frowned at any of my preposterous similes to the lives of the masters. He stood looking at me quietly, thoughtfully. "Ah," he sighed at last, "if you could put half that amount of passion on canvas you would be a real artist."

"Monsieur," I retorted, "if I put nothing on canvas but spend my time talking instead, I will never achieve anything."

"Passion and determination are essential," he went on apparently without hearing me. "In my opinion Lautrec had no talent, but he had a passionate desire to portray life as he visioned it—rough, seamy, sometimes grotesque. He was a true artist. He *made* himself become an artist."

The man seemingly was lost in his thoughts. He no longer talked to me alone but to himself as well.

"Dare to be different—that is important!" His fist crashed into open palm as he paced back and forth on the rooftop. "Impressionism. What did artists know of impressionism until Lautrec? Nothing. He dared to be different."

His eyes blazed with a passion for art as he talked of it. I literally jumped as he turned to me and demanded, "How old are you, Mademoiselle?"

"Just past twenty," I stammered.

"A year older than Picasso when he came to Paris to study. You have talent, and Picasso then had only determination—determination plus passion! He had a passion for learning, for experimentation, for everything at once."

He stopped and glared at me. I was just a student interested in perfecting a few art principles. I loved to paint, but I was not obsessed by it. I couldn't force myself into becoming a cubist like Picasso, nor could I really appreciate his abstract art, no matter how important it had become. I merely wanted to express beauty, to make use of my gift. I had neither passion nor determination to become great, and I knew it—if no one else did.

"What do you want of me?" I asked with suddenly found vigor. "Who are you, anyway?"

He roused himself from his personal thoughts and smiled at me again.

"Ah, I frighten you. I am sorry. You are very young, and I forget. First, let me explain that I am a friend of your instructor at the School of Arts. He asked me to talk with you when he learned we live in the same apartment hotel. He has great faith in your ability, but he feels you need an incentive or you will miss the height which you might achieve. Still, he did not want me to influence you because of my position, so I did not give you my name."

"What *is* your position?" I demanded. "What *is* your name?"

"I am Jean Luis Du Bon." He turned then and made his way toward the stairs.

"Monsieur Du Bon," I gasped. "I didn't know..." He was one of the best known and most copied contemporaries in Paris.

"In years to come," he was saying, "there will be other forms of art—forms which have not as yet found expression. Who knows by what names they will be known? But they will be important. Try to find yourself in them."

"I will certainly try...I don't know about achievement. My first concern is quite personal. I desire a good life, based on certain principles, and my spiritual achievement means more than an attempt at fame."

He gave no credence to my words. I doubt he heard them, for he had delivered his ultimatum, and if I were the person he thought I was I would heed it. He gave me a final smile before disappearing through the doorway. I saw Monsieur Du Bon a few times after that. Always he was distant, though courteous, and I found myself wondering if he had forgotten the conversation we had shared on the rooftop.

— — —

Now, fifteen years later, Monsieur Du Bon remembered me. "I am married now," I heard myself saying, "with three children. My name is Radley, and I still paint quite a lot. I have won some 'first's,' but I'm afraid I will never be important in the eyes of the world. I'll never be a Lautrec or a Picasso."

"Ah, who knows?" he mused. "Perhaps you will be a Radley. You are still young. Your art has begun working for you, according to your club president, Mrs. Ashby. She tells me you have sold over 200 paintings in the last five years and have received considerable recognition in your region. In fact, you are one of the reasons I am here today. Following my lecture I understand I am to present you with an award for winning first place in a national contest in which one of your paintings was hung."

Pop and op art had gained a great amount of attention and popularity in our part of the country, along with abstracts. I had merely tried to keep apace of the trends.

"I have seen it," Monsieur Du Bon continued. "Your work is showing more passion. You still have promise of unused talent, if you will delve deeper and make it work for you."

Those words again—make it work for you. I thought of the considerable "talent" I had used along with elbow grease in decorating my home, and of the pleasure my family and I shared in the atmosphere of muted colors and corresponding accents throughout the house. I thought of my studio and the hours I spent there creating a landscape, seascape, or still life for a friend's house, or a wedding gift. It seemed to me that such talent as I possessed was indeed working for me, in unexpected ways.

"Now tell me of your painting," he insisted. "Do you spend much time in pursuit of your destiny? It is so vital, the time spent!"

My destiny? My time? "Well, yes. . .but you must recall I told you long ago that my personal pursuits, my happiness, my philosophy of life would shape my destiny—not the development of *one* talent." I remembered the hurried chauffeuring of my children about town this morning and the good-bye kiss I gave my husband as I sent him on his way to exercise with a golf ball. It seems I spend a great deal of time in pursuit of my destiny, I thought. "Yes," I agreed again. "Quite a lot of time."

"And what of your media? Do you still work mostly in oil?" he asked, not really listening to my words.

"Oils and acrylics. I use them almost exclusively." But I have branched out now. I use poster paper and ink for Cub Scout projects and crepe paper for birthday parties. Even knives, sometimes, for jack-o-lanterns.

Polly Ashby found us in the lounge still talking about art. As she hurried toward us, gushing adjectives over Monsieur Du Bon, I thought of her chiding me for being late to so many of the meetings, and realized that had I been on time more frequently I might have known of this particular lecture by this particular man. I was sorry it had come as a surprise to me, for I knew that tomorrow, after he was gone, I would think of many things I should have asked him. Now all I could do was shake my head yes or no to his queries. However, by being late I had had the opportunity of talking with him alone, of remembering my early years, of having a special "nudge" at self-evaluation.

It was a surprise, too, that I had won the national contest . . . and I made mental notes to act as stunned as I had been on first learning of it from Monsieur Du Bon. I would not have to *act* pleased for I was, without doubt.

"Oh, I see you two have met again," Polly was saying.

"I had no idea, Virginia, that you knew so accomplished a man until he mentioned you this morning. Why haven't you told me? Monsieur Du Bon belongs to the world now, you know. He is quite famous. It was only by the greatest stroke of luck that we were able to engage him for our club. He was in the country anyway, attending a showing of his works, so we asked him to take a day off to come here. He was reluctant at first. Seems only at the last minute he agreed to lecture and to view our exhibit."

I tuned her out. His being here was part of my destiny, as it had once been to meet him on a rooftop in Paris. "It is a shame you have children," he had said. "They take so much valuable time away from your creative hours. Such interferences. I had hoped you would dare to be dedicated to your talent alone; still, if you do not allow your family to demand your attention when you are working, you can accomplish much."

"Oh, I am accomplishing much," I had replied. "In fact, I am working on three masterpieces now. You told me fifteen years ago that it might take a long while to achieve my heart's desire, but that perseverance and determination were the true factors of success. Well, I have these in abundance now. My work is difficult but very rewarding. I intend to take years in finishing these creations."

"So . . . I am pleased," he said, as Mrs. Ashby took him by the arm and led him to meet the group of artists and lovers of art.

I would not have been able to explain or to defend my own life. He was of a different mold than I—a man who had no thought of "building *first* the kingdom of God" and then awaiting all the marvelous things that could

41

influence human life. It might take a much longer time to achieve my ultimate goal than had I chosen his way, but no great work could be done in a day. I would expect to keep on winning honors with my paintings. I might even achieve more national recognition, but my passion would always be as old as the world, without a single new discovery. One of my works would have to spend several more years wearing braces on her teeth so they would be straight and beautiful. Another would have to outgrow her lopsided grin and the trace of freckles on her nose. The third . . . well, that would be more of a challenge than the others. He would have to learn to sit quietly once in a while, to curb his mischievous impulses that could be so trying to sitters and teachers, and I would be the one who would help mold him into the lovable, dignified, achieving son he would become.

I would always continue to paint because I knew I was given some talent, but I would never have the determination to create on canvas the masterpieces that might be recognized for more than a lifetime. My masterpieces would be too busy discovering talents of their own.

The Birdwatcher

She placed her hat, with its pink rosebuds and pink veiling, carefully on the bureau. Every Sunday after church Mrs. Collins placed her hat carefully on the bureau. If she did not tuck it away in a box in the closet she could more quickly put it on top of her tightly knotted hair when her son arrived to take her for a drive after dinner. She did not want to keep him waiting.

Most Sundays he took her out to dinner along with his wife and two young sons. But more often than not she was glad when they did not ask her. The children were noisy, and her daughter-in-law always seemed tired, as though keeping an orderly home for a husband and two sons was almost too much for her after a half day's work in an office. Spoiled, these younger women! Too many conveniences could rattle them. She was pleased to eat a snack alone today in her own pleasant apartment, and then enjoy the drive with the family. She hoped her daughter-in-law would sit in the back seat with the boys.

Mrs. Collins hummed a hymn as she put a kettle on the stove for tea. It was one she liked especially, and now that there was nobody at home to hear her, it didn't matter if she enjoyed a hymn or two. She liked attending church now, too, though she still refused to attend her son's congregation so he wouldn't know that she was there every Sunday.

She smiled to herself as she put a linen napkin beside china already laid out on the little round table in the bay window. She supposed most people liked to attend church when they got older, especially if they were alone as she was.

Pete Collins had been a good man during his lifetime, struggling in his priesthood work without her support. He had needed people and friendliness and interesting episodes in his life as she did, but she had always been jealous of his church activities in which she could not participate. So Pete had had his routine and she had had hers, and she had never shared religion with him. He had been gone almost seven years now. She was past seventy herself. My, time had a way of flying!

The church was only half a block away, and she met such fascinating people there. She especially liked the young pastor because he was so friendly. He reminded her of her little brother Bert who had once wanted to be a preacher. Well, she had taken care of that! Thirty years as an engineer was much better, in her opinion, than being under church appointment. Bert seemed happy enough, though she couldn't understand why he wanted to support the church financially as he did—so many things he could have had for himself and his family if he didn't spend all that time "caring and sharing," as he called it.

Mrs. Collins spread her lunch on the table, then picked up her binoculars and looked out the window. The large bay gave her a good view up both sides of the street in either direction. Her son had given her the binoculars several years ago so she could watch birds in the many trees along the shady street. Too bad so many of the fine old elms were dying and being cut down. The park department men had said it was Dutch elm disease. Well, it was killing a lot of the trees, all right, and this diminished the number of the birds in the neighborhood.

Mrs. Collins dabbed at her napkin to get the juice from an apple tart off her fingers. It would be time soon for her son to arrive.

To the right was a wonderful view, now that the last diseased elm had been removed. She could see all the way to that widow's duplex, the one who led the choir at church. With her binoculars focused just right she could distinguish who it was the widow was entertaining for Sunday dinner on her patio. From this height, the view over the brick wall was excellent.

Was it?—yes it was. It was the pastor. "Thought that woman had something up her sleeve," she muttered aloud. "I saw her smile at him sort of special when the choir finished singing. Ought not to be a pastor until he gets himself married, I'd say."

Mrs. Collins felt that she was getting to be quite an authority on human behavior in the neighborhood. Like the young girl in the third house to the left of her bay window. She had known quite a while before the girl eloped with that skinny boy they would be getting married. Magnified contours from this height told her lots more than meeting a person on the street. Once she had felt sorry for the girl and almost offered her friendship when her parents neglected her. Well, thank goodness she hadn't gotten involved! Those parents seemed to feel bad now, but what had they expected, letting her drop out of school and run the streets the last two years?

The boy seemed like a good kid—for a poor, uneducated person. They would probably make it when they had their own home and family, even if the going would be rough because of little money, limited education, and no guidance from their parents. That was no concern of hers, of course.

A limousine of ancient vintage rolled up the street and turned in the drive across from her. Mrs. Collins focused the glasses on the car and then on the occupants as they were helped out by a chauffeur as ancient as the automobile. Most of the fine old homes along the once-shady street had been turned into apartments, but two maiden sisters still maintained their "town house" with an abbreviated staff of servants and their decaying genteel life. Their country estate had been sold years ago.

Mrs. Collins watched the sisters enter their tightly shuttered house. They always attended church across town where the people with money had long since moved and built an elaborate house of worship. Then they came home again to their darkened windows, shutting out the sunlight and the reality that times had changed a lot of things.

Too bad they seemed to feel impelled to put up such a front. Mrs. Collins supposed they kept their windows shuttered downstairs so that any visitors would not be able to see faded colors and frayed fabrics. Provided they ever had any visitors! She certainly would never visit that pretentious pair.

If visitors could look into the upstairs windows, as she could, they would be surprised. She knew this was where the sisters really lived, with their worn furniture and a sparsely laid table which they shared with their chauffeur/handyman/gardener. There they were now, in matching smocks which they wore most of the time—to save their clothing, she supposed. Hmmm, cheese and crackers again, milk, apple wedges, and some kind of a casserole.

Mrs. Collins welcomed the air and sun and view beneath her own windows. She reached over and pushed back her dainty white curtains a bit so no breeze would be closed out. The birds chattered among themselves in the treetops. Life had been good to her in the old days, when she and Pete were young. But it was still a good life without him, when she was no longer young. Yes, a good life—just lonelier. If she could start over she might make friends somewhere. . . .

She turned the glasses slowly, sharpening the view for distance again. Now, what was that widow up to? She had stuffed the preacher with good food and now she had him stretched out on a hammock. Looked as if she might be reading to him.

Closer, something crashed on cement. Drat! She couldn't see across the street two houses to the right. That huge elm was in the way. The Harrises were fighting again. She laid the binoculars down and leaned forward to listen. It would be much more interesting to watch. Come to think of it, she had noticed a couple of dead leaves in the top branches of that elm—too bad to lose another tree, but she would have to report it to the Park Department first thing tomorrow morning. The tree was definitely dying. Better to cut it down now than to let it infect others near by.

The bell sounded, and Mrs. Collins jumped up. Oh, dear . . . she had let more time slip by than she had intended.

"Come in," she called. "Come in, son."

He stood just inside the apartment door, sniffing the aroma of apple tarts appreciatively.

"Glory, son, you look more like your father every day. I suppose you preached this morning. I'll be only a minute, but long enough for you to have a tart. My hat's right here on the bureau." She looked admiringly at the pink wisp, glad that once more she was seeing a hat or two at church on Sunday mornings. Eventually she would be in style again . . . and she did so love beautiful things.

"Been up to your old tricks, I see," her son ventured while he munched on the pastry.

"Old tricks?" A wave of guilt spread over her as she appeared in the bedroom doorway with her pink veiled hat dipped jauntily over one eye, the rosebuds trailing along her tightly drawn hair.

He grinned. "The binoculars."

"Oh, yes . . . the binoculars." She smiled at him sweetly. "I am truly fascinated," she said, "by all the birds around here."

The
Day
Aunt Nettie
Died

Looking back now, I find it hard to believe that fifty years have passed since Aunt Nettie died. We met her when I was ten and my sister was twelve. We didn't know then that Aunt Nettie was a talented and shrewd woman with a sense of humor, a spinster with scores of male admirers, and—above all—a lady. To us she was simply a relative with whom we were to make our home after our parents were killed when one of those new automobiles crashed into their buggy.

Aunt Nettie was in her early sixties when we went to live with her in her Victorian home. Only once did she mention the accident which had left us dependent on her. It was the week we arrived at her home.

"Girls," she said with her soft throaty voice, "I am your father's aunt. Your own great aunt. We are brought together by an unhappy circumstance, but this need not keep us from being happy." From that time on neither of us realized any unhappiness while we were with Aunt Nettie. In fact, I doubt either of us had a single thought of our own after that day . . . no questions were tolerated, and no explanations were given. We were at her mercy, and somehow it seemed right.

By the time my sister was eighteen and I was just past sixteen, we were allowed to "entertain" so long as we were always together. We had picked up a few of Aunt Nettie's endearing ways but not, of course, her versatility. No one could match that. Her wit and charming personality were attributes we both needed and tried very hard to imitate; however, this was not to be. She was the lamp; we were the moths.

Aunt Nettie could switch her mood from coy to matronly to helplessness in a matter of minutes, according to the requirements of the persons she entertained. She played chess, dominoes, and bridge equally well, and sent her challengers home the losers of nearly every match yet feeling that somehow they had won. Aunt Nettie enjoyed her popularity. She loved people—she loved herself first and most; she loved dependent people like my sister and me; she loved those who worked for her, and people who attended her church, and those who belonged to her clubs. Especially she loved the balding, paunchy bachelors who hinted they should have met her years ago, and the tired, sad-eyed widowers who pursued her openly, pleading their causes with insistence.

Always gracious, always kind, always full of fun— and always the perfect lady—Aunt Nettie did have one incurable fault. When it first became known to my sister and me that a flaw might possibly exist we tried very hard to ignore it or to explain it away. Finally it became so pronounced we had to acknowledge it. It was understandable, of course, and looking back now we can see that it was probably why we patterned our lives after hers. The fault concerned the men in her life: *she loved them all.*

It was as impossible for Aunt Nettie to select one man over the other as it would have been impossible for her to choose which she enjoyed most—her morning cups of chocolate or her afternoon cups of tea. There was a delightsomeness about both of these to her. As well as a special need for each. If it was difficult to choose between chocolate and tea, how much more impossible to choose which man would be more desirable as a husband.

Aunt Nettie's last evening was spent rather vigorously—for her. "Do have some more popcorn, Harvey," she insisted. This gave her a chance to turn her attention to Clyde and Edmund, whose glasses of root beer she kept filled.

"Now if one of you gentlemen feels like playing chess, I'll be happy to lead."

Over the chessboard Aunt Nettie pressed for information concerning a former admirer.

"What do you hear of George? Is he really going to marry the widow he has been courting since last fall? She seems so young for him."

"Oh come now, Nettie," Harvey managed to exclaim past his new teeth and the popcorn. "George is twelve years younger than you, so you've no call to get jealous. The widow he plans to make his missus is only ten years younger than he, so she's not a whit too young for him. She'll take good care of him if he gets down."

Nettie didn't pout; she was too proud for that. "Well, I wish them every happiness of course. And I'm *not* jealous, Harvey. However, I shall miss George next summer; he has kept my shuffleboard court painted, you know."

"No harm in asking them both to enjoy a game with

you and the girls, Nettie. It might get the court painted again."

She did not give Clyde's comment any credence. Everyone who knew her understood that Aunt Nettie would share any of her possessions willingly, freely—her money, her time, her company—all but her men. In the next room where my sister and I sat reading and listening, we smiled at each other. Poor Clyde. He would be marked off the list now, with his preposterous suggestion.

Aunt Nettie always maintained her dignity. It was quite proper for her to dismiss players when the conversation had begun to lag and she had won the queen.

"Dear me," she said. "Suddenly I feel a wee bit dizzy. That root beer you brought tonight was excellent, Edmund, but maybe stronger than usual."

The gentlemen snapped to attention and assisted her to a slipper rocker heaped with pillows. She smiled her thanks in her most gracious, "feeling poorly" manner. She leaned back after Edmund plumped the pillows, Harvey spread the afghan over her knees, and Clyde held her hand. My sister and I stood in the doorway, smiling at these marvelous old gentlemen.

Aunt Nettie thoroughly enjoyed these last moments as reigning queen in their lives. When she sighed and closed her eyes, none of us realized that she had gently but definitely loosed the silver cord binding her to earth. Perhaps she knew, for she did not struggle. Aunt Nettie had always looked forward to the next world with both curiosity and anticipation. She had always said she was confident there was more and better ahead. "I've given enough material gifts to others," she had once said, "that I'm sure the Lord will stack that up against my self-centeredness."

The thought that Aunt Nettie could be self-centered was incredible to us. Surely she had jested!

By the time it occurred to the gentlemen and to my sister and me that Aunt Nettie was no longer hearing words of solicitation, it was too late to obtain stimulants for her failing heart. In fact, Edmund was a bit bothered because of the strong root beer he had brought.

"It couldn't have hurt her, could it?" he pleaded. "I made it myself from good clean roots."

"Of course not. It was delicious," my sister said.

"Did we tire her with too many games?" Clyde wanted to know.

"Of course not. She was delighted you were here to challenge her," my sister replied.

"She really enjoyed the evening," I assured her friends, as Aunt Nettie herself would have done.

Finally someone had presence of mind to call a doctor, and all of them stood by my sister and me until Aunt Nettie was taken away. Then the three men—shocked and grieved—left too.

"This is an unhappy circumstance," my sister said.

"But it need not keep us from being happy," I answered.

My sister and I still live in Aunt Nettie's Victorian house, spending her money and playing her games. Nothing much has changed for us since she went away except that the suitors who call are ours now. Unlike Aunt Nettie's solitary rule, our men friends must be shared because there are two of us. Times, too, have changed. . . but that doesn't affect us much. We often watch television rather than play games, but there are still lonely persons who need to play chess or dominoes and who like to share a bowl of popcorn and a pitcher of root beer.

Now and again we speak of Aunt Nettie because we loved her, but we are careful never to let the unhappy experience of her death keep us from being happy, as we feel certain she would wish. Rather, it seems quite appropriate to remember that last smile on Aunt Nettie's face—as though she were employing her most pleasant wiles on Saint Peter.

Mary Jutness and Her Prize

Mary Jutness was quite sure she was a loser. She felt she had been a loser as far back as she could remember, which was most of her nineteen and one-half years. As far ahead as she could foresee, things weren't likely to change much. Her sister, Inez, had been born beautiful. She had been born simply mediocre—she knew this because her parents and her sister had told her frequently. Her sister had a multiplicity of talents, but Mary really couldn't do anything outstanding.

Such things didn't matter a lot to her anymore, because she seldom allowed herself to think about it. She was as happy as most people she knew, though a little less involved, perhaps, for one her age, and with quite a lot more leisure time than most of her friends. Her sister had been very popular while growing up, and Mary lived in her sister's shadow until finally Inez got married. Then things settled down a bit. When she thought about it, which she hardly ever did, Mary knew she had one good thing going for herself—she always smelled good.

Smelling good had become a matter of pride, although she really hadn't had much to do with it herself.

Ever since she had outgrown dolls she had received perfume for every birthday, Christmas, and other special occasion. What else was there to give a plain girl who never went anywhere or did anything dynamic? When she thought about it, she realized that she had a bedroom which could vie with the cosmetic counter of most neighborhood drugstores. On every available furniture top, bookshelf, and counter space were perfumes, colognes, scented soaps, skin creams, skin softeners, mist sprays, hair sprays, and bouquet powders. This depressed her occasionally, so she didn't spend much time thinking about that aspect of it—just how good she smelled!

Where she worked (the Harvey Harrison Brown Insurance Agency) Mary was general file clerk. It pleased her to hear comments such as "Mary has every file at her fingertips," "Mary surely has a remarkable memory," or "What did we ever do before Mary worked here?" She didn't believe the comments, because she had known since early childhood that she didn't have anything great to offer the world—but it was nice hearing such compliments anyway. She had decided long ago, when she grew old enough to realize that she had never had any encouragement at home, it was because she was born without the usual redeeming qualities most people had. This made her feel sort of apologetic about herself.

"It isn't my memory at all—just a good cross file," she would explain modestly. She felt certain that the secretaries (and sometimes even the bosses) lingered in her filing room not so much to give compliments on her work or engage her in conversation—what could she say to interest them?—but because she smelled so nice.

"Guess what's new now," one of the typists said when Mary arrived at work one Monday morning. "We're getting an efficiency expert to straighten us out and shape us up."

"I won't be bothered by 'straightening out and shaping up,'" Mary declared, "so long as he doesn't bawl me out or foul me up." She felt suddenly insecure; it would be very difficult to take criticism about her work because it was so important to her. It was something she felt she could handle.

In a few days there he was—sitting right outside the door where Mary kept the files. She was glad she smelled especially good when he was introduced to her. Not that it mattered, but he had such nice eyes—though they didn't miss much—and his smile was nice, too, even if he didn't smile often. Mary was sorry that he had a cold (his eyes watered and he sneezed twice) but she was too shy to mention it or say "*Gezunheit.*"

"Rumor has it that the supervisor is designing a special medal himself to present to the best worker," a typist informed her.

"I'd rather have money," Mary said. "Where would a person file a medal?"

The typist laughed. "What would you spend it for—more perfume?"

In the following weeks Mary hadn't much to say to the efficiency expert. After all, he was quite important, and she was just a file clerk. She did notice, however, that he watched her a lot from behind his desk, and she felt that he listened to the conversations when people asked her for files or lists or other information. Mary knew she always looked neat, but she couldn't assume he was actually watching or listening to *her*, with all those dazzling secretaries sitting close by. It must be a habit of his to stare straight ahead when he was thinking. That would account for it.

"And what system do you use?" the efficiency expert asked one morning, looking over her shoulder.

"Well, I growl at people a lot. They don't call me 'Scary Mary' without reason," she answered with a twinkle in her eyes. Then she wished she hadn't attempted to joke with him, because he hadn't laughed at her comment...and because cute remarks didn't exactly go with the Lady in Spain perfume she was wearing.

"I doubt that. I've noticed that you're one of the best liked persons around here," he remarked. "No one seems to move without checking with you." Mary didn't believe that, but since the efficiency expert didn't get huffy at her humorous attempt, she took a deep breath, gave him a quick grin, and explained her filing system in detail.

"You're pretty young to be in charge of the files, aren't you?" he wanted to know.

"When I first started working here it was a part-time Vo-Tech job—you know, with high school credits attached. After I was graduated the regular file clerk I had helped decided to get married and move to another city. I sort of inherited the job."

"Ever think about college? You seem to have a quick mind."

"Yes, I've thought about it," Mary said. "But right now this is the job I like—the space I want to occupy. I *am* taking courses at night school in accounting, so I can change sometime if I ever get tired of this job."

The efficiency expert wanted to know one more thing.

"Did you inherit the filing system, too, when you inherited the job?"

"Oh, no. Well, not exactly, I mean." Mary wished she had worn her Lilac Mist at Dawn. "I used the basic plan but improvised the former Warner System quite a lot, including the addition of a complete cross-file reference which was really my own." Then she explained the former system and why she had thought it was inadequate and how she had found a need for specified files. "I hope I didn't do wrong in changing things," she finished hesitantly.

"On the contrary, your perception and expertise indicate your extreme value to the job, and indeed to the company itself. I will have very little to suggest in my report."

The efficiency expert went away then, with one of his rare smiles on his lips. Although Mary wore a different cologne every day, he didn't come into her room again. He spent his time asking questions of the secretaries and typists who buzzed around him like bees around a pot of honey. Mary could understand this, of course; they were all so attractive, and she was plain—medium dark hair, medium dark eyes, medium height, medium weight— just mediocre.

Then one day the employees began to talk about plans for a company dinner where the medal would be given to the most efficient worker, and lists of recommendations would be given to everyone on how to improve his/her service to the company. The efficiency expert had finished his work there. Mary knew that the desk across the aisle would seem vacant indeed without him in it.

"You've won the medal, Mary. No doubt about that,"

a secretary assured her. "Everybody has known it for weeks."

"Everybody has known it but me," Mary said. "I haven't been told about winning anything, and the efficiency expert hasn't been in my filing room enough to know what I do. He only asked questions one day, and he wasn't feeling well then. He acted as if he was coming down with a cold or something."

"Don't kid yourself. He knows what you do all right—he stares in here all the time through that open door."

"Oh, he's just staring into space while he is thinking," Mary said.

"Listen. We've all been watching him, and he has been watching you."

Mary couldn't help being pleased with those words even though she didn't give them credence.

"No wonder," the secretary sighed. "No one can compete with you. You are the most attractive girl in the office, the most intelligent, the most willing to help everyone. You have the best personality, the best sense of humor—need I go on?"

Mary didn't know what to make of the secretary's comments. They were so unusual, so unanticipated. . . . Suddenly she looked down at her pale blue sweater over the gray tweed skirt. She was glad she had chosen this outfit today because even her mother, who was seldom complimentary, suggested it was rather becoming. And of course she was glad she had worn the right perfume to complement it.

The efficiency expert came into her room just before quitting time Friday afternoon. "Who are you going to the dinner with tonight, Mary?"

"No one. I always go places alone." She hoped he

wouldn't notice her blush. For the first time it bothered her that she did not have a date.

"Then why don't we go together?" he asked.

"You mean...you and me?"

"Yes, I would like that very much." He hadn't seemed to notice how startled she seemed. "I know you must be very particular, but I would be honored if you would allow me to pick you up at your home and take you to the dinner."

Honored? She liked him for that most of all, though it was difficult to believe.

"That...that will be just fine," she stammered, trying to force her voice to be calm, though daisies were blooming and bluebirds were singing inside her.

"I'll be by at seven sharp," the efficiency expert said, as they synchronized their watches. "It will be nice talking with you all evening. You have so much to offer those around you...by the way, if you can find the time, perhaps you can help me this weekend with a group of junior high boys and girls I'm working with who are studying "Creativity and Self Worth" at my church. But you can decide that later."

He wanted help from *her?* Oh, yes! She could organize the group, categorize the study materials, keep the achievement records. Maybe she could even learn a little about those subjects herself.

"Oh, and one other thing," he added.

"Yes?" She held her breath so he wouldn't know how fast her heart was beating.

"Please be your own sweet self. I'm allergic to perfume."

The Second Week

Heat shimmered up from the highway as Neva stepped off the bus. She tightened a strap holding her tennis racket to the side of one of her suitcases. . .and sat on the other. Fine thing! A million miles from nowhere, and the only connection with civilization was fast becoming a speck on the horizon.

Neva read with annoyance the roadsign, "RLDS Reunion Grounds—3 miles." Lucky I wore sneakers, she thought, no longer able to see the disappearing bus. She surveyed the gravel road leading to the camp. Her view of the landscape was breathtaking—nature's beauty at its best: green grass spotted with wild flowers, and trees reaching up into a cloudless sky.

"Marching order, trail scouts. Fall in," she shouted to the four winds and a startled pair of meadowlarks. With an exaggerated salute and a scuffle of suitcases she began walking—only slightly hampered by the bulkiness of her load.

Although she had a healthy body and vigorous spirit, Neva looked like an uncertain teenager when Mark Simms stopped with a screech of brakes and a swirl of dust.

"Hi," he called as he climbed out of his eight-year-old compact. "You the waterfront supervisor for reunion?" He flashed a welcoming grin, and his blue eyes assured Neva that he could be trusted.

"Sure am," she replied, as she handed her suitcases to him.

"If you'd waited where the bus stopped I'd have picked you up sooner. I'm returning from town, and I was supposed to be waiting for you at the highway. I just didn't make it as soon as I thought I would, and when I did get there you weren't." He grinned again, and Neva was conscious of his long glance at the brown wind-blown hair and the dust-covered face beside him.

There hadn't exactly been apology. In fact, missing him seemed somehow to be her fault, but Neva smiled as though the whole situation were perfectly normal. Didn't everyone trudge down a gravel road at some time?

"I suppose you're Mark Simms. I have a letter from the camp director saying you'd meet me. I'm Neva White."

"I've heard about you," Mark answered. "You're Brother Rugger's granddaughter, aren't you?"

"Yes, and he is the one responsible for my coming here. I'm not a member you know. My mother married 'out of the church' and moved away from any affiliation."

Mark's grin was spontaneous. "You'll like us," he assured her.

Neva's dark brows formed a frown as she thought of the new experiences before her. Would she really like these people? In high school it had been easy to evade questions about religion. Her dad wasn't a member of any church, and her mother's church—with headquarters in Missouri—had meant little to Neva. Religion hadn't even been a topic of conversation among her university friends. Her mother had wanted her to attend a church college someplace in Iowa, but she simply wasn't interested. She had been too busy with athletics to worry about theology.

"My granddad asked me to volunteer as waterfront supervisor," Neva explained. "I have a Phys Ed teaching position at Pleasant High this fall, so he thought my 'talents' might as well be used during the summer."

"Well, I vote in favor of his idea. He hit on a good one this time," interrupted Mark.

"Oh, I know him. He's a sly old fox. He's planning to 'convert' me while I'm here," Neva laughed. She looked at Mark with a mischievous twinkle in her eyes. "He has been concerned about my lack of religion since I was a baby, I think."

Mark's usual grin was lacking. In fact he looked almost somber as he turned into the reunion grounds and pulled to a stop before the main lodge. "All joking aside, Neva, I hope you *are* converted to the way of life we advocate. But don't overestimate your granddad or anybody else. No one can do the job for you—or wants to; you'll have to convert yourself."

Meeting granddad Rugger again after nearly four years away at college and getting situated in camp was exciting—though time consuming. It was after supper before Neva saw Mark again. He was standing outside the lodge talking with a group of young people.

"I'll see you later, granddad. Mark is motioning me to join him." Brother Rugger nodded his approval and watched with appreciation the acceptance of Neva into the group.

She found that a half-hour of fellowship could slip by seemingly in a few moments. The sun was beginning to send long streaks of gold and rose into the turquoise sky when Mark took her hand and drew her away from the others. "Come on. I'd better show you the equipment before it gets dark."

They headed toward the recreation equipment storage shed. "The first Saturday of reunion is when people start arriving in large numbers, and some of the children will be wanting you to let them go swimming before they settle down to the routine of classes. This will be a new experience for all of us. Usually our reunions are only one week, but the committee decided to try an experimental two weeks this year especially geared to family needs."

"Good. I like being busy, and I was hoping that since this is a reunion of your church people it wouldn't mean all study and no play," Neva replied. "I'll be ready for the onslaught of kids."

The first week of reunion was one of conflicting thoughts and persistent unrest for Neva. She attended classes and heard sermons, but she could detect no strange doctrines. Many ideas were new to her, but analyzing them after stretching out on her cot at night, she found they made sense. She wished now she had spent at least a little time in developing some spiritual insights. She had felt that good health, an appreciation of good books, right living, and the glories of nature were enough. Now she wasn't at all sure she had not missed an important facet to her personhood. Her grandfather somehow ceased to be a relative and became a source of wisdom for her as he seemed to be for others who sought his counsel daily. Most important, what Mark said was true—no one was trying to "convert" her. She was merely a part of the body, reaching toward a mutual goal.

She spent morning "free times" teaching fundamentals of behavior in the water to youngsters. During afternoon lessons the teenagers were anxious to learn new strokes or to perfect old ones. And the evening swims before campfire service were relaxing periods for young and old alike—that is, except for Neva. She was concerned as she watched these families play, worship, sing together, and she couldn't understand the burden which seemed to rest upon her. When she taught a new swimming stroke she found herself saying, "This is the way you should do it, but no one can do your job for you. You must practice and master it for yourself."

One morning in the second week of reunion Neva was aroused by a tapping sound. At first she thought it a knock at a dormitory door, calling someone for early study. When she struggled to full consciousness she realized she was in the heart of a woods at a reunion site.

The tapping went on. Stretching and yawning as she went, Neva walked out into the open to look for the woodpecker responsible for the disturbance. Whoever heard of walking before reveille? That woodpecker must be part buzzard to be so mean.

The morning air was invigorating, and the day promised to be a particularly beautiful one. In the distance she could perceive the first stirrings of the kitchen crew preparing breakfast. Well, now that I'm up I might as well make the most of it, she thought.

Guess I'll surprise granddad by showing up at the morning prayer service.

With that thought in mind, Neva began to get dressed. She could visualize in her mind's eye how surprised her grandfather would be . . . if she could keep from telling him before then! In fact, it would be fun to see Mark Simms' reaction, too, since he had stopped asking her to go to the prayer services after the first few days.

Neva purposely walked into the service tent a little late and noticed with girlish contentment the exchange of glances between her grandfather, who had just offered the opening prayer, and Mark, who was leading the music. Smugly self-satisfied she found a seat near the back of the tent.

At first the meeting seemed unusual to her. She could hardly understand people rising to pray aloud before so many others. Then, as she listened to their words of commitment, she seemed to forget personal fear. She noticed Mark smile at her with special friendliness as he announced the next song. As the voices swelled together into one fraternity of praise she understood his thoughts: "In this old, old path are my friends most dear. . . ."

The balance of the service was lost in detail to Neva. She vaguely knew she had stood and given her testimony before these people she had come to know, but she could not actually remember what she had said. She knew only that somehow things seemed right and plain to her, and the most important feeling in life was to be a part of this great bond of loving and caring that held more tenderly yet bound more closely than family ties.

By midmorning she had made up her mind about a lot of things which had confused her for nearly two weeks. She hurried over to the concession stand to find Mark as soon as the swimming lessons were over.

"Mark, I need to talk with you a moment." Neva's throat felt tight, and she wanted him to know the emotions she felt too deeply to express.

His reassuring grin showed he understood. "I told you that you'd like us," he said.

"Oh, yes. I do," she answered with sincerity. "But I want to tell you something," she went on.

"I know. The diamonds in your eyes this morning told me. Let's go find your granddad." Mark's hand held hers, and at that moment the whole world seemed wonderful.

Brother Rugger, coming out of the lodge, saw the couple and waited for them.

"Granddad," Neva said, "I want to be baptized. I want to be one of you."

The words did not seem strange for a granddaughter to say to a grandfather. They were said simply, humbly, as he himself had said them nearly five decades before.

Nails, Snails, and Puppy Tails

No one had ever drowned in Honeycomb Lake, and so far its waters were unpolluted by waste or debris. It was far enough away from industrial centers that no acid rain had ruined the area, and those who owned property were proud of their lake and countryside. And those who lived there year round, like the Ramseys, especially loved the quietness and beauty of the surroundings.

If her husband had asked if his two brothers in college, or even the three teenage sisters, could spend the summer at the lake with them Claire would have been delighted. Instead, Earl Ramsey had suggested that his two youngest brothers visit them. Claire was the first to admit she knew nothing about boys. She felt inadequate to cope with ten- and twelve-year-olds. Especially boys.

Riding with him to the bus stop to pick up his brothers, Claire found time to put her questions into words. "What shall I expect, Earl?"

He grinned at her. "Just two ordinary kids."

"You know what I mean," she persisted. "Are they like the familiar Dennis, or two Charlie Browns?"

"Just very ordinary boys," he repeated. "Looking for some summer fun."

Claire didn't quite know how to explain her reluctance at having them all summer, so she stopped talking. Their silence stretched out along the country road, with only Earl's occasional whistling to break it.

Through the trees Claire could see the lake shimmering in morning sunlight, now looking golden. The lake was blue, of course, but when the sun shone on it the rippling water turned to gold and looked like a giant comb oozing with wild honey. This was how it got its name—Honeycomb Lake.

A winding road led around the lake to a highway. In the winter Earl and Claire drove twenty miles into town every day where Earl taught math in high school and Claire taught kindergarten. She loved the little people she taught, each one, but the girls were really special. She had been an only child, separated and shielded from other children. When she met Earl, the eldest of eight children, she loved everything about him, including his large family.

"Come on, honey," Earl was calling her back to the present. "Cheer up. All you have to do is treat the boys nice—as you do me."

"As I treat you? With all the goofy things I do they will think I'm a clown."

"Don't you believe it. They'll adore you. *I* do."

This had been the beginning. It hadn't been until later, after the boys had been met and greeted, brought home and fed, that Claire began to feel real apprehension about the summer. They were as different as two peas from the same pod possibly could be. Twelve-year-old Roy was dark, intent, and quiet. Todd, who was ten, talked on and on, his sandy hair bobbing with his exclamations.

"You two fellows go along with Earl and investigate the waterfront while I do the dishes," Claire suggested after lunch. "The three of you will need to get re-acquainted. It has been a couple of years since I dragged Earl down the church aisle, you know."

"Roy can go with Earl. I would rather help you," Todd said.

"Aw, come on." Roy was irritated with his younger brother. "You'll just get in Claire's way."

"No I won't either. You like to talk to me, don't you Claire? Besides," he glared at his brother, "you know I don't like the water."

Claire's eyebrows literally went up at this bit of news, but she found herself saying, "Oh, that's all right, Roy. You go on with Earl. I'll be glad for Todd's help."

"Well, if it's okay with you. . . ."

"Sure it is." She was furious with Earl for just standing there and not helping her out. As the screen door slammed shut she said "Now, Todd, are you really afraid of water? Don't you swim at all? The lake is about all we have here for entertainment."

"No, ma'am. I'm not afraid of it . . . I just don't think it is much fun to swim, that's all."

Claire laughed. "Are all ten-year-olds as honest as you?"

"I guess so," Todd answered, looking serious for the first time, and a little apologetic.

"Well, we'll just dunk the dishes right now instead of you, and we'll all be happy." In the back of her mind Claire was trying to figure out what on earth to do with him. An entire summer without swimming left a lot of hours to be filled some other way. If he were younger he wouldn't be a problem—she knew very well how to handle kindergarteners.

During the next week Todd stuck close to Claire's side, while Earl and Roy spent every available minute in or on the water. When she did take dips Todd sat on the beach making designs with twigs or building roads in the sand. He played quietly until she came back to sun herself beside him. Then he began to talk—his favorite pastime. She glimpsed a young mind, saw dreams, realized aspirations as she never had before in a youngster. She was fascinated, and found she could relate to Todd on a one-to-one basis instead of categorizing him into some preconceived pattern.

"If you learned to swim well you would like the water. Let me teach you," Claire would say repeatedly.

"No, thank you," he always answered tight-lipped. "I'm not a water person."

"Well, we will just have to plan some special things for you, then. I want you to have a good time this summer. Is there anything you'd like especially to do?"

"Nope. Mom told Roy and me we weren't to make any extra work for you."

"Fun things wouldn't be work, Todd."

"Yeah...I guess not."

He dismissed nearly all of Claire's ideas. When she talked with Earl about it he said to forget it. "The kid is having a great time doing just what he wants to do, which seems like nothing. Roy told me they have both passed their junior lifesaving at the Y, so Todd can swim all right. I think he just isn't interested in the sport."

"Okay. I'll stop nagging him."

Earl laughed as he stooped to kiss her. "To tell you the

truth, lady, he's got a crush on you."

"A crush! Are you teasing?"

"No, I'm quite serious. It is an honor, you know. It's probably the last time he will like any female until he hits the teens."

"Oh, Earl, that scares me. What should I do?"

"Nothing special. It's a normal reaction with kids. Just be understanding. My special love at that age was my fourth grade teacher—whose name I no longer remember."

Claire tried to be understanding indeed. While Earl and Roy spent their days boating and swimming, she and Todd fished and walked and put puzzles together and pitched softball. Todd helped by getting the barbecue grill ready for her and by gathering wood for the fireplace from the area behind their home. They would have a terrific pile of wood for the winter. After the first month, Earl surprised them all by renting bicycles for the rest of the summer.

The days passed quickly, melting into one another in the sunshine. Honeycomb Lake oozed golden ripples, and a soft breeze wafted pleasant cooking odors around the lake. The rain was cooperative—coming only during the night and leaving quickly with the first streaks of dawn.

"I need to get some supplies," Earl announced after breakfast one morning. "Shall we all go into town?"

Ordinarily it would have been a good idea, a day out, but Claire had awakened tired. It seemed she was more tired after the night's sleep than before she had gone to bed. "You take the boys and go. I'll rest today."

"I'll stay with Claire," Todd announced, hurrying outdoors. He didn't put in an appearance again until after Earl and Roy had gone.

"If you don't mind I'd like to lie here on the couch and read a while," Claire told him when he came in.

She awoke with a start. Todd was putting a puzzle together quietly across the room. "My goodness, it must be lunch time."

"Sure is." Todd's sandy hair bobbed as he got up and came over to the couch. "And it's all ready. I did the dishes, and then I made some sandwiches and got out some potato chips. I think most of those chips are gone, though, 'cause I've been eating them." He grinned.

"Oh, fine. Now, I'll just make a pitcher of lemonade, and after lunch we can go boating. How about it, pardner?"

The lake was very quiet, and it looked blue again as they set out. "This is fun, isn't it?" Claire shouted above the motor. "Let's explore the cove at North End."

They noticed the lake surface change first, ripples alternating along its deep blue spine, changing to gold. Then they noticed clouds skudding quickly across the sky, shutting out the sun.

"Hey, we're going to have a storm," Claire shouted. "Let's get back quick."

Todd, who was always agreeable, nodded.

The lake was not too large to make it back to their dock before the rain started splashing into their faces, but the waves were deepening fast. Claire felt her stomach churn. "What a stupid thing to happen. I'm sick."

Todd moved cautiously beside her. "I'll help. We're almost there."

"Here, keep her in line," Claire shouted, cutting the engine down as they neared the dock. She leaned over the side and vomited. She felt so silly. Then she felt a jolt as a wave slapped the boat broadside. She was leaning too far out, to vomit again, when another wave slapped hard. . . .

— — —

Claire opened her eyes. She felt very tired, and wanted to go back to sleep, but something tried to focus her brain to attention. "Is that you, Earl? What are you doing here?"

"Yes, honey. Everything is okay. Just rest now."

"What happened? I feel so funny." Then she remembered the storm, and Todd trying to secure the rope. "Where's Todd?" she gasped, trying to sit up.

"He's here. He's fine—just drying out."

"The storm came up so fast, and I got so sick. How did I get here?"

"My kid brother saved your life, Claire. That boy is a real swimmer. He secured the boat just as you fell out of it. Then he jumped in and hauled you out of the water. He was scared because you had struck your head, and you were being carried out by big waves, but he knew you were all right, so he rolled you up on the sand as soon as he could swim back to shore. Then he headed for town on his bike."

"Now I remember. It seemed like a dream, but mostly I was aware of what was happening. Is Todd okay? Are you sure?"

"Yes, he's fine. We were on our way home as he got halfway around the lake, so we ditched the bike beside the road and came on to find you."

Outdoors the lightning still flashed, but Claire felt at peace. All was well, and her little brother-in-law could actually swim—just as Roy had said. She was lucky he had the strength to fight the waves and get her onto the shore.

"Honey, Dr. Litton is here now," Earl was saying. "I called him out to look you over, to see that you're none the worse for this experience."

Claire smiled weakly. She heard him tell Earl to wait outside for a while, and then he began his examination. "We want to be sure there is no concussion. Have you noticed the nausea before? How often do you waken tired? Mr. Ramsey tells me you weren't up to par this morning."

The questions went on. Claire was never sick, everybody knew that. It must have been the motion of the boat on the water. No, she was seldom tired, but recently . . .

The examination and questioning came to an end. "I've been so busy this summer with the boys. . . . I didn't think to come in for my regular check-up . . . is it really true?" Claire rambled on, wanting to sleep again, but feeling excited now.

"You call in a day or two and make an appointment, Mrs. Ramsey," the doctor said.

"Thank you, doctor. I'll be in right away."

She heard the door close and the car motor start, then a knock on her own door.

Earl came in, flanked by two small boys with big eyes. "You feel up to having company for a minute or two?"

"Sure. I'm likely to conk out—the doctor gave me something to make me relax." She turned to Todd. "You saved my life, little brother. Sorry I missed seeing you swim, but I'm sure glad you could. Thanks."

Todd's face burned red with the praise. "I couldn't let

anything happen to you, Claire. Next to mom . . ." he flung himself on the bed and hugged her. Over his tousled sandy hair she smiled at Earl and Roy. Then she went to sleep again.

Claire awoke with the sun streaming in the windows and the smell of bacon permeating the house. Earl had forgotten to put on the exhaust fan, and she felt nauseated again. She lay back, shutting her eyes hard and squeezing her stomach muscles tight. In a few minutes the feeling passed, and she got up, put on her robe, and walked out to the kitchen.

The three looked startled, as though she were a ghost. "Hi, honey," Earl stammered. "We were trying to be quiet and not waken you. We were going to surprise you with breakfast in bed. How do you feel?"

"Great. Just great." Claire reached for the exhaust fan as inconspicuously as possible.

"We can still bring your breakfast to you in bed if you go back," Roy faltered.

"Or we can sit on the couch and all eat off the coffee table," Todd suggested.

"Yes, let's do that. Earl, you dish up for us so we will only have our own plates. Roy, you pour the juice and milk. Todd, you place the chairs."

Earl chuckled. "She's okay, boys. She's her old self again when she gives orders like that."

After breakfast the boys did the dishes. Earl was perturbed about the doctor's comments. "Other than assuring me you didn't have a concussion, he just seemed noncommittal. I've been worried about you."

"My fault. I asked him to wait until after I've been to the office and had a thorough examination and he runs some tests. But there seems to be nothing out of order, so

77

why speculate? I thought it would worry you less for him to be noncommittal . . . so that was my idea."

"So long as you are feeling good, that's all that counts. When is this office call to take place?"

"I'll call today and see. Frankly, the days have gone so fast I haven't even looked at the calendar for weeks. Now it is nearly the end of the summer, and the boys will be leaving us. What is today?"

Earl walked over to the desk and checked the date. "It hardly seems possible, but this is Saturday, August 7. Another two weeks and they will be leaving for home. *We'll* be going back to school too."

Claire could hardly believe it. Losing Todd and Roy after such a surprisingly wonderful summer made her feel lonesome. She had found out a lot about boys she had never suspected. They were really human after all.

"Earl," she said, "a lot can be said for 'sugar and spice and everything nice' but it isn't half as interesting as what little boys are made of."

They all drove to town on Tuesday. Earl and the boys shopped for school supplies while Claire kept the appointment with Dr. Litton.

"Will it be all right to work a while, doctor?" Claire was anxious to keep occupied.

"Yes, but I would suggest that Christmas would be a good time to quit, depending on the school rules, of course."

Claire walked along the sidewalk to the car. The others were not back yet, so she window-shopped a little, looking wistfully at the designer jeans. When she saw them coming she met them at the car.

"How's everything?" Earl asked anxiously.

"I'm on top of the world. Perfect heart. Perfect lungs.

Perfect blood. And perfect appetite. Where shall we eat?"

The boys laughed, settling into the back seat.

Earl drove to a small restaurant on the edge of town. "Sorry, boys, no drive-in for hamburgers today. We'll have a family-style meal of fried chicken, because that's Claire's favorite.

Claire experienced another wave of nausea at the odor of food, but it passed quickly. The four of them ate hungrily and had a good ride back home.

"I'm going to rest again," Claire declared, kicking off her shoes and reaching for sandals as soon as she stepped inside the door. "I must be getting lazy."

"You've been through a lot. A person doesn't nearly drown every day," Earl sympathized.

"I'm going for a swim," Roy announced.

"Me too." Todd had been talking school all day, though his actions toward Claire were still fiercely loyal. "There aren't many more days for me to swim. I'd better catch up."

"We'll watch you from the porch," Earl assured them. "Don't go out too far when I'm not with you."

Now that they were alone for a while Claire hardly knew how to tell Earl the news he should certainly know. She looked at him, sprawled out in a reclining chair. He looked so young and relaxed, without a care.

She followed his gaze to the boys. They were racing, both swimming swiftly and expertly. They looked hazy, like golden streaks in the Honeycomb.

"Earl . . ."

He turned to her then. He was still young, still relaxed, but with a care after all.

"I know, Claire. At least, I think I do. You look different, sort of excited and contented at the same time."

"Dr. Litton and I talked a lot. I told him about being a lonely little girl, and lining up all my dolls and pretending they were my babies. Then he talked about how fine your two brothers are, and I confessed how frightened I had been at the beginning of the summer and how now I love them so much I don't want them to go. . . ."

Earl interrupted. "But what did he say about you?"

It was impossible to keep the news longer. Laughing, Claire got up to sit beside him in the large chair so he could still watch the boys. "Why, just what you are thinking, dear. With the Lord's blessing we'll have a girl—or maybe. . .just maybe—a boy."

Summer Cheat

Sarah's fingers typed five full lines in flying staccatos before she realized her mind wasn't on her work. She proofread the typing and found she had made two mistakes in the first sentence.

"That makes the third letter you've torn up this morning," Vicki Dawson observed. "What are you trying to do, become a perfectionist?" Her smile grew as she watched Sarah wrinkle her nose and give a big sigh.

"I'm just not with it," Sarah complained. Vicki was Sarah Warren's new-found friend, and Sarah would have enjoyed confiding in her . . . but that was impossible. Sarah felt she could never confide in anyone again—except Larry, of course. It had been Vicki who had introduced her to the office personnel nearly three months before. It was she who had taught her how to prepare advertising layouts and had made her feel like one of the group immediately. Well, *almost* like one of the group. . . .

By noon Sarah was glad to have an hour's respite. She knew Larry would be waiting for her in the lobby, and she was glad about that, too. As soon as the elevator door slid back she hurried out.

"Funny girl," Vicki murmured to the others. "She

81

would be real nice to know if she didn't always carry a secret burden. I've tried to help, but she won't let me."

"Maybe *that's* the burden," remarked Irene, the file clerk, as she watched Sarah and Larry go through the swinging doors together. "I'd like to have someone like him on *my* mind."

— — —

Sarah smiled at the message Larry had written across the tabletop with the moisture from his limeade glass. "Larry loves Sarah."

"You're no help at all. Be serious." She pretended crossness, but reached over and patted Larry affectionately. "Really, what *am* I going to do?"

Larry's deep-set eyes closed and he brushed his short beard thoughtfully.

"The way I see it," he began with slow deliberateness, "you'll have to tell him today. You needn't be afraid of him because he is your boss. Pretend you're talking with your father . . . lay it on the line."

"That is exactly why I feel so terrible, Larry," Sarah wailed. "I haven't told my father, or my mother. No one knows but you. I'm beginning to feel so sneaky lately I'm surprised you can still like me."

"*Love*," corrected Larry. "I'm surprised at what you did, but that doesn't change the way I feel about you. When I've finished law school I want to make a home with someone human enough to make mistakes once in a while."

"You deserve more, Larry," she whispered.

"Let's say I don't want to settle for less," he said.

The two blocks back to Advertising, Inc., were all too short. "I'll have to go right in," Sarah said, glancing at her watch.

82

"Okay, but don't forget," Larry insisted. "If I can hold out for four more years in college, you can make it through two—so get it straightened out fast. You'll feel a lot better." With this last word of advice he turned quickly and walked toward the corner drugstore where he worked during the summer.

Sarah tapped her nails nervously on the top of her desk. Wasn't this just her luck! Mr. Bruce wasn't in and the big office clock already showed a quarter till two. One more half hour and every ounce of nerve would be gone for a confession today.

She put fresh paper in her typewriter and started drafting the Moran tire ad again. She was nearly finished when she saw Mr. Bruce come down the wide aisle toward his office. *Now*, Sarah thought, and she started to speak to him. Then suddenly she felt her voice would only squeak. She smiled instead. I'll let him get settled first, she decided.

"Sarah, would you look here a minute, please?" Vicki was needing a little help on baby crib sheets—sometimes just a word spoken aloud to someone else made the whole thing fall into place. Please, not now, Sarah thought, but she felt a certain amount of relief as she realized this was an excuse to put the confrontation off longer. This should take at least ten minutes if she kept talking to Vicki. . . .

"Miss Warren, please come into my office." Mr. Bruce was speaking on the intercom. Sarah wanted to run in the other direction, but habit caused her to smooth back her hair and check to see that her blouse was tucked in properly as she walked toward the closed door.

Sitting behind the huge mahogany desk with a view of

the growing city at his back, Mr. Bruce looked up as she entered.

"I'd like to talk with you, Sarah." She accepted the offered seat with a smile and hoped he wouldn't notice the pulse beat in her throat.

"Are these rumors I've been hearing about you true?"

Oh, horrors! Why haven't I told him the truth before he found out from someone else. This is much worse than if I'd told him.

"What rumors have you heard, sir?" She barely breathed, waiting for his answer.

"Why, this boy who's going to be an attorney."

"Oh!" Sarah's expended breath almost choked her. "You mean Larry," she affirmed.

"Is it true you are planning to marry this young man?"

"Yes, after he completes his law studies. That's not for four more years," she finished weakly.

"And what does he think about your schooling?" asked Mr. Bruce.

"Well, he wants me to continue." *Tell him, Sarah,* her conscience shouted. *Tell him you have every intention of going back to school. Tell him you lied when you applied for your job. Tell him, tell him!*

Mr. Bruce's voice was quiet. "How do your parents feel about it?"

"They want me to go back to college."

"And how do you feel about it yourself?"

Sarah felt the flush of blood creeping up into her cheeks and forehead. "I'd. . .like to go back, too." *Oh, honestly, Sarah, what a coward you are! It's one thing to lie to get a job for the summer, but not owning up to it is detestable!* "No," she said resolutely. "It's more than that. I *want* to go back."

It seemed years before Mr. Bruce responded, and then he spoke as though Sarah knew what was in his mind.

"Your young man has four more years before he finishes his schooling. Then it will take several more years for him to become established. If you went back to school for two years to finish your degree, and worked here summers, it would still give us a lot of your talents... with the possibility of future part-time work at least."

"Sir, I don't understand. . . ."

"Sarah, we need you in Advertising, Inc. So far this has been a small business in a small town. Now things are on the move—the town is growing so fast the population has nearly doubled in the last three years. We need the best advertising we can produce and that requires knowledgeable, well-trained personnel." Mr. Bruce rolled a pencil between his palms. "I'm offering you summer work next year if you go back to college... and a job for as long as you want after you graduate. I've watched your progress. Few persons can learn advertising as quickly and apply it as well as you have done."

"Oh, Mr. Bruce, how wonderful!" Sarah's relief was surpassed only by her happiness.

He nodded at her reaction. "Advertising, Inc., needs to expand, and we plan to choose the best workers we can get. It is imperative that they be well trained."

"I'll certainly try to live up to your expectations, Mr. Bruce."

As Sarah walked back to her desk she made a pact with herself. I'll not only live up to Mr. Bruce's expectations of me, she vowed, but more important—I'll live up to my own. I will *never* cheat again.

The Birthday Gift

"Today...is *my*...birthday." Skip, skip, hop. "Today...is *my*...birthday." Hop, skip, skip.

Timmy was singing to himself as he jumped over the swinging rope firmly clutched in both hands. This was the day he had waited for ever so long. He could hardly remember what last year's birthday had been like, except that he had spent it with Mrs. Logan instead of at home with mother and daddy. Mrs. Logan was very nice, and he had good times at her house, but somehow he always felt that he was being punished when he had a sitter. He was so big now—five years old today—he shouldn't have to have anyone look after him. Even changing the term from "baby-sitter" to just "sitter" didn't help much.

"You should be very glad for such a lovely person to take care of you when I am not with you," Timmy's mother insisted. "You always tell us about the adventure stories you hear and the fun you have when you're with Mrs. Logan."

"Yes, I do, and I like Mrs. Logan...but I like you better," Timmy had replied. "Besides, I'm old enough now to do baby-sitting myself."

Mother just smiled when he made statements she did not agree with.

It was really Shelly's fault. If it hadn't been for Shelly he would have had a wonderful birthday last year and again this year too. He got lots of nice presents last year, and he knew he would get some nice things again today. But, there *was* Shelly, and he couldn't do anything about that.

Last year daddy said, "Shelly is your nicest birthday gift." Timmy tried hard to be glad about having a baby sister, but it was hard to think of Shelly as a gift. It was hardest of all to know that now *his* day was *Shelly's* day too. The thought of sharing birthdays with a sister every year forever was almost more than a boy ought to have to accept.

"You're older—you must be gentle with the baby," mother told him.

"Why?" Timmy asked.

Mother had looked a little surprised at his question. Then she smiled and said, "Daddy is larger than any of us, yet he is very gentle with us. It would make him very unhappy to know that one of us was hurt or injured in any way. Having a good family life, with love and happiness, is the reponsibility of each of us; we must share gently and caringly with each other. Do you understand?"

"I think so, mom."

"Because you are bigger than Shelly, you should enjoy helping show her how to walk, talk, and to keep her from hurting herself in any way."

"Yeah. I understand. Kind of like Jesus."

"Exactly. He is our example."

Timmy tried hard to be gentle and caring.

"How's my big boy?" daddy would ask when he came home from work. "I'll play with you in a minute." Then he would pat-a-cake with Shelly while Timmy had to wait his turn.

I hope birthdays get better, he was thinking. Maybe this year I'll get something I want.

"Timmy...Timmy, come here, dear!" Mother called.

In just a moment Timmy had hoppity-skipped up to the back steps. "Here I am," he said, carefully wrapping his jumping rope over the handlebars of his tricycle.

Inside, the kitchen was bright with sunshine. Good smells were in the air, and Timmy's mouth watered.

"You have been playing so hard all morning I'm sure you must be hungry," mother said. She was pouring a glass of milk from a carton in the refrigerator. "Wash your hands while I get some of these fresh-baked cookies to go with the milk."

Timmy grinned. Mother looked so pretty in her pink and white checked apron. She looked pretty, and she kept her hair short and curly. She didn't wear jeans all the time like some other mothers, and Timmy liked that. Shelly called "Tin-Tin" to him as he passed her play pen. She had a pink and white checked bib around her neck, which matched mother's apron.

Um-m-m, how good the cookies smelled, fresh from the oven. Timmy took a big swallow of the cool white milk and then bit into a golden cookie with pieces of chocolate melted inside.

"This is yummy," he complimented his mother.

Timmy liked the way she surprised him with good things to eat. She always seemed to know when he was hungry, even sometimes before he knew it himself.

"Will you please pass this cookie to Shelly?" mother asked.

"Sure."

For some reason, Timmy liked doing things for the baby.

Shelly crawled toward him as he stepped over to her pen, then got up and ran around in circles. She blew bubbles in her excitement at having a cookie. "Tank-u," she said politely at mother's insistence.

"She's kind of cute—for a girl," Timmy admitted. Then, remembering that mother did not allow him to make remarks against Shelly, he talked fast so she would not correct him. "Say...I don't have to get another sister for my birthday this year, do I?"

Mother laughed, although Timmy couldn't see anything funny. "No, dear," she answered. "Daddy will be here in a few minutes with your gift. I'm quite certain you will be delighted with him."

"Him? Aw, not a brother!" Timmy wailed his disappointment. "I want something my very own. You know, something I can play with."

"No, not a brother," assured Mother. "This gift will be your very own."

"You must remember, Timmy, that when you alone own something the responsibility for it is yours," daddy said from the door.

Because he had been eating cookies and thinking about his birthday, Timmy had not noticed the car turning into the drive or his daddy coming into the house.

"I know, daddy," Timmy said, running to hug him. "I don't mean to be 'difficult' as mom says I am sometimes. I just want to be happy."

"I understand," daddy assured him. "Mother and I

90

realize the problems you have by sharing your birthday with Shelly. So we thought someone else might help you a bit. Come outdoors and see him."

Cautiously Timmy followed his father. Who else, he wondered? He glanced back to make certain that mother was coming outdoors too, with Shelly.

Not a sister, not a brother . . . who could it be?

At first Timmy did not see anyone. He looked all around. Then he noticed his jumping rope was missing . . . only another boy could jump rope! Then he saw it, wrapped around the collar attached to a little ball of black and white fur. Fur! His gift suddenly came alive then with a wriggly tail and tiny yaps.

"Oh, daddy . . . a puppy!" Timmy dashed toward the furry animal with shouts of joy. "Really, mom? For my very own?"

Daddy answered. "Mother and I will help you, of course. Shelly will learn to love him too, but we will all depend on *you* to care for him. He is yours."

Shelly stretched down from her mother's arms and tried to pull the soft fur in Timmy's arms.

Carefully Timmy disentangled Shelly's baby fingers. "You're bigger—you must be gentle with our puppy," he told his sister.

The
Talent
Scout

Buzz Harriman was troubled by some nagging thought which didn't come clear in his mind.

Today, or perhaps another day within the week, would bring his lucky break—the one he had waited for so long. The sun was shining; he had married a girl with a savings account; and his agent was one of the best. Everything should be "turning up roses." Still, he was troubled.

"Relax," Chuck Wise had told him no more than an hour ago. "Just remember to be on your best behavior—no, more than that—be *better* than yourself for one week. Then you'll have nothing to worry about that I can't handle for you."

Chuck couldn't be expected to understand how a guy's stomach could knot up when he wasn't sure of himself. . . not sure of the impression he would make when it would count most. Chuck was an agent, not a would-be star. He hadn't had to fight for everything he ever got, to step on other people if that's what it took to get on top, to smile when he wanted to spit, to stand around in theater "barns" autographing programs for stupid people.

"Look," Chuck had told him, "You're getting a

chance every other country singer is trying for, so don't blow it. I had to talk fast, because frankly, Buzz, you're not all that good; but I *did* it. I tried, and I got you the chance. Plenty of singers have more charisma than voice. Pops Larseni has given me his word he will listen to you sometime this week. You can't afford to flub this one, Buzz—neither of us can!"

Okay, so he didn't have the best voice in the world—but it had never been better. The show was packing in a lot of people...there was no complaint from any corner. So why did he have this gnawing in his stomach? It reminded him of how he used to feel when he was a kid and held on to the money his dad had given him to put in the collection plate at church.

Chuck was right—he couldn't afford to blow it. He might not get another chance like this. It would take years to build up again, if he ever could.

"Remember," Chuck had cautioned, "Pops is rocket. If he likes what he sees and hears, you'll orbit. If he doesn't like you, you'll splash down all the way."

"Yeah, I know. So 'don't be nervous' you tell me. Just 'be better than myself for one week'," Buzz had mimicked.

"Right. You've got it, Buzz, out there beyond yourself somewhere. I should know if anyone does—I'm the one who has worked with you, tried to re-do you, tried to latch hold of that better person I know has to be around somewhere in that psyche of yours. Well, anyway, that's why I stay with you. In a couple of years—with a lot of hard work and without the drugs—you could be another Elvis."

Buzz had been contrite for a few moments. "Guess it's

just the odds that bother me. What if the whole thing goes flat?"

"Think about it," Chuck had replied quietly. "If it goes flat you can still entertain and enjoy what you're doing. You don't have a great need for material things—your wife can buy those for you—so it is just your ego that would get hurt. Plenty of people try and fail. It doesn't make them less in anyone's eyes. . . they just don't become *more.* Get me?"

"Are you trying to let me down easy? You think I can't do it?"

Chuck had sounded angry. "I *know* you can do it if you can just get past yourself, Buzz. Your voice is okay, and you have a really good chance. . . if you can control your temper and disregard for other people. Be careful. Pops is crafty. He has more tricks up his sleeve than Double-o-Seven."

"A mean guy, huh?"

"No, not really. He's honest about it. When he scouts for a star he fakes a job for a day or two as a stage hand, a door guard, or handyman in the neighborhood. I remember when he was scouting Merrilee last year. He posed as makeup man so he could observe her reactions to the people around her."

"Well, there's nobody new around here," Buzz had growled. "I've looked everybody over. . . I know them all."

"What about that girl who's been hanging around mooning over you?"

"She's nuts about my singing, that's all. She's scared to speak to me when she gets a chance. Besides, Pops couldn't disguise himself as a girl!"

"You're right there," Chuck agreed. "Those big eyes

and skinny legs definitely are teen. But keep your eyes open . . . and act happy."

Buzz was alone now, headed for his dressing room. It was almost showtime.

"Oh, Mr. Har-ri-man!"

There was no mistaking that squeal. Buzz hunched his shoulders and hurried on, pretending not to hear. One thing he didn't need right now was a groupie monopolizing his time.

The girl dashed up beside him, breathless. "Oh, Buzz—I mean, Mr. Harriman, I thought I would *never* catch you alone. Could I have your autograph?"

He managed a weak grin. "Other people aren't poison, you know. I can sign with more than one person around me."

The girl giggled. "But this is so much more romantic. You know, sort of intimate. Just knowing you're signing your name for me alone is won-der-ful."

"Yeah. Well, here's the name. See the show sometimes," he quipped. "It's the box office cash that counts with me."

"Oh, I do see the show. I mean, I have—five times already!"

"That's what keeps me in business," Buzz muttered. What more was there to say to a kid like this? He pushed past her and hurried on toward the dressing room.

"Mr. Har-ri-man . . . ," she called after him.

Buzz stopped and glanced back. "Look, kid, I'm in a hurry. I've got a lot on my mind."

"I just wanted to say thanks."

"Yeah, okay." Buzz hurried on feeling kind of sorry for her—living on other people's glory you might say. Another time he might have talked with her a while, dazzling her with his charm. But today might be his big chance. He couldn't be wasting words on a teenage "bag of bones" today.

Nancy Larseni held up the autograph to her father. "Sorry, daddy," she said. "I tried to keep him talking longer, but he wouldn't cooperate."

"You were great, Nancy," he answered. "I was right behind you in the wing. I could see him and hear him—almost thought once he had seen me, I was so close. His expression when he turned away from you was... interesting!"

"Don't tell me, daddy." Nancy giggled. "I bet it wasn't complimentary."

"No matter," he answered. "He was in a hurry. Funny about that...he won't be going anywhere."

A Bite
of Eve's
Apple

The cab slackened speed and turned into a narrow lane where a sign indicated we were entering "Dust Pan Beach." I fumbled in my handbag for sunglasses, found them, put them on. The tinted glass shaded my eyes from the glare of sun on water and sharpened the focus as I watched for cabin numbers.

At the end of the lane I could see a small clearing forming an area shaped like a dust pan. The rounded edges of the pan were fringed with palms and flowering shrubs. The straight edge scooped out to the ocean, and was lined with a dozen or more identical cabins along a rim of beach. Beyond was the endless expanse of gray-blue water.

The cab driver followed the one-way drive and slid to a stop at Cabin No. 9.

"This is it," he said curtly.

I discovered the number painted on the curbing. "Yes. . .so it is." I got out and pressed five one-dollar bills in the driver's hand. "Keep the change," I said.

"What change?"

"Oh—Isn't that enough?" It had not occurred to me

that Florida taxi rates could be higher than in New York.

"It's okay." He grinned, took off his cap, and scratched his balding head. "Where do you want your bag?"

I was looking at a sign attached to the front gate. *Beware of mean dog*, it warned. I did not see a dog behind the white pickets, but the sign made me sufficiently apprehensive...I've always believed in signs.

"Just put them here by the gate."

The cabby replaced his cap, gave a salute, and dropped the bag at my feet. "Good luck," he said. "You'll need it."

I glared after the retreating car. I hoped I didn't look as though I needed help on this assignment. The newspaper ad circled in red stared back at me as I read it once more:

> Woman, 20 to 30, to share cabin, Dust Pan Beach. Bus service to Miami. Divorcee. Call 722-5600.

I had telephoned and talked with the divorcee—a short and decisive interview. I was to stay one afternoon and night with Catherine Todd-Baker (but everyone called her Carrie), and if we got along well we would make permanent arrangements. Carrie hadn't mentioned the dog.

The gate swung easily at a touch and colored pebbles crunched noisily underfoot. On the narrow porch another sign warned, *Wet Paint*, although the cement had never seen a paintbrush. I decided to walk around to find another entrance.

I was not prepared for the first view of Carrie. She was on hands and knees scrubbing the back stoop, and all I had was the diminutive rear view of some faded blue shorts with tanned legs and bare feet under them. She had heard me coming around, so she stood up and grinned. The front view wasn't much bigger or better than the back. An over-sized sweater enveloped the top half of her petite body, and her head was swathed in a large towel.

"I'm Sabetha Norris. I called you about sharing the cabin."

Large brown eyes looked me over from head to foot. Then the corners of her eyes crinkled, her lips curved up, and her whole face became radiant.

"Sabetha? What do people call you . . . Beth?"

"Sometimes."

"You'll be *Sabe* here."

"All right. Whatever you want—it doesn't make any difference to me."

Carrie laughed. "Well, come in. You'll want to see the place. Don't mind stepping on the clean floor; it will look more like a home with footprints. Since you braved the 'mean dog' and 'wet paint' without complaining, you won't be afraid of the rest of the nest."

"I didn't find either," I countered.

"Not likely to," she returned, with another smile but no explanation.

Now that she had started talking I had the feeling she wouldn't turn off soon.

The cabin had a large living-dining room facing the ocean, and I discovered that the back door was actually the front door. She called the doors landside and oceanside. Beyond the living room area was a room with twin beds. The tiny bath had a shower but no tub. Beyond the dining area was a kitchen just large enough for two persons to cook without bumping into each other.

Carrie went out for my bag and unpacked it while I sat helplessly watching. When she took over, there seemed to be nothing to do but watch.

The unpacking completed, she unwound the towel from her freshly shampooed hair. It was long and deep auburn. By comparison my own looked like stacked straw. Freckles dotted her nose, and full lips curved easily into a smile.

"I like you already," she confided. "You're the first *nice* person Mrs. Baker has sent to check on me."

In the silence which followed (Carrie had made a pronouncement rather than an accusation) I could hear the roll of the surf and the sharp cry of a sea gull.

Sounding like an afterthought, I stammered "Wh—what do you mean?"

She looked at me unwaveringly, and I could not keep my determination to play the game. "Yes, Mrs. Baker did send me. But I am on your side—if that helps."

"Then why did you agree to spy for her?"

"A number of reasons. I was bored working for her—reason number one. It seemed like a good chance for a paid vacation—reason number two."

I was appalled by my own candor.

Carrie started preparing dinner. "We'll talk about it later."

The grateful look I gave her was premature.

"You might just tell me," she said, pausing in her preparations, "who he is."

I did not follow her thought. "Who *he* is?"

"The man in the office. Is he your boss?"

She was positively psychic. It was true I had left my

job because of a man. "Yes. I was secretary to one of the junior executives," I found myself answering. "Mrs. Baker hires a staff to do her own advertising, you know. When she heard I had decided to quit, she contacted me about coming to Miami for her."

I was reluctant to tell her my troubles, but she let the subject drop without further questioning. "I knew you were not the type to spy by your own initiative."

I was glad she felt that way. After all, I had been sent all the way from New York to find out everything possible about Carrie, and so far I knew nothing. A complete zero. On the other hand, she already knew why I was there and that I had left my job because of a problem. I think it might have been embarrassing to explain, this far away from the cause of my trouble, that my magnified discomfiture in my employment could have been handled, I felt, with one stony look from Carrie.

Our entire evening together was pleasant. Carrie was an excellent cook, an intelligent conversationalist, a lively but comfortable person to be around.

— — —

It seemed I had hardly laid my head on the pillow when I was awakened by a persistent sound I could no longer ignore. Glancing across the room I found the other bed empty. Hurriedly I pulled on my robe and opened the blinds to see what the commotion was. The bright sunshine assaulted my sleep-laden eyes, and at first I could hardly see.

"Stop honking that horn," I called at last. "What on earth do you want?"

The cabby took his hand off the horn and stepped out of his cab. "Well, are you ready to go?" he called back.

He was the same driver who had brought me out the previous afternoon.

"I'm not going anywhere. Who sent for you?"

"Nobody. I had another fare out this way and figured I'd haul you back and save you having to call me out again. It will be cheaper for you."

"Wait a minute." I closed the blinds again.

I dashed through the kitchen, out landside, and down the walk to the cab.

"Now," I panted. "Please tell me what this is all about."

"Seems I was mistaken. I thought you'd be ready to go back to the city."

"I'm trying," I persisted, "to understand why you thought I'd be leaving."

"They all do. A new girl has been out here almost every day for the last two weeks. And Miss Carrie gets rid of them fast. That's all."

"You know Carrie?"

"Sure. Every cabby in Miami knows Carrie."

Every cabby in Miami? What had I gotten into? "I see," I said, not seeing at all and hating my personal thoughts. "Well, I'm not leaving. At least, not yet."

The man grinned. "Well, so long."

"So long," I echoed as he started the motor. "And thanks anyway."

He gave me another salute, then left in a swirl of dust. It had settled again on the flat, paved roadbed before I moved away from the picket fence.

Rounding a corner of the cabin, I could see Carrie far down the beach. She seemed to be digging into the ocean with a net, close to the shore, and putting shells into a bucket. What was she, anyway, a beachcomber?

She waved when she saw me, picked up her bucket, and ran to meet me. "Deviled crab for lunch today," she exclaimed, brandishing the bucket.

"Is that what you were doing? Digging up crabs?"

She laughed, and her face lit up like the morning. She didn't look like what I was beginning to think she must be, although I wasn't exactly sure how those persons were supposed to look when they were outside bars or dark streets.

"I thought I was chasing them," she said, "but maybe I was digging them up. I have hundreds of times."

I tried to question her as we walked back to the cabin. "Am I going to stay on here for a while with you? Do you like me well enough, knowing that Mrs. Baker employs me, to try sharing your cabin with me? Do you . . . do you have many visitors?"

The smile disappeared, and she said nothing until she had deposited her bucket of crabs on the oceanside stoop, washed her hands—a bit too thoroughly I thought—and poured two mugs of tea.

"I'd like you to stay," she said between sips. "Only I haven't completely planned my strategy yet."

"Your strategy?"

"Line of action. Suppose you tell me first, Sabe, just what your job with Mrs. Baker entails."

I could feel my face getting crimson. "Oddly, I'm not sure except to spy on you, as you pointed out last night. Then I am to make a daily report to her, or if everything is quiet, a two- or three-day report. About anything unusual, anybody who comes here to see you . . . that sort of thing."

"Do you know why?"

"No. Mrs. Baker said you were—quote, poor relation,

unquote. She wants all the information I can accumulate concerning your habits, friends, life-style. . . ."

"And especially any indiscretions, no doubt?"

"Yes. Especially those. What's it all about, Carrie? Is she trying to cut you out of an estate settlement or something?"

"Simple, really. She wants to cut me out once and for all from her son's life. I once was married to Aaron Baker, Jr."

"You mean *the* Aaron Baker?"

"Right. Formerly of New York, recently of any port in a storm so long as it is as far away from Carrie Todd-Baker as his mother can persuade him to go."

"That's pretty high on the totem pole, Carrie. Wow!"

"I know." Carrie smiled a smile which wasn't quite so dazzling now. There was a flicker of pain in her eyes, and I knew she still loved the man who had been her husband.

"So goes the world, Sabe. At least some of it. Another mug of tea while I get breakfast?"

I took both mugs and refilled them. Something did not add up. It was probably better to just out with it, so I did. "Carrie, why did you advertise to share your home if you knew Mrs. Baker was trying to 'get something on you'? Also, what good does all this do if you and her son are already divorced?"

"Ron still loves me, and I still love him. This is a real threat to her. Aaron *always* did as he was told—it was a rigid part of his training—and when she said 'divorce' he did. But he is not happy that way, and as soon as he grows up a bit more he will know his own mind. I am suggesting that he will be as determined as his mother once he gets the feel of using his initiative."

"So you are having to fight off innuendoes and anything she can dig up?"

"Yes. My idea is to invite them all in to meet me so *I* can watch *them*. I knew sooner or later I would find someone like you."

"But if she continues to watch you. . .and my days may be numbered here by *her*, not you. . ."

"I know. She was having me shadowed, running me ragged with door-to-door salesmen, surveyors, you name it. That is when I decided to learn what I could by having her flies come right into my parlor."

"Thanks. I deserve that!"

"You were the first 'fly' with gossamer wings instead of germy feet."

She was frank and refreshing. I liked her, and found myself intensely disliking "pompous Baker" as we had secretly referred to Agatha Baker at her *Couturiere Shop*.

"I understand from reading recent social columns in the Miami newspapers," Carrie went on, "that she has found a new love for Ron. It looks as if she wants him to marry Sylvia Newby, of the Newby-Wilson fortune, but she strongly suspects that her little Ronnie might have memories of young love. So, Carrie must be spied on."

I was furious. "She needn't think I'll report anything against you. I won't do it!"

Carrie knew I meant what I said. "It's good to have an ally at last. . .but I *want* you to report. Between us we ought to be able to supply her with all sorts of interesting stories, which fortunately cannot really incriminate me."

"I'm with you all the way."

"Thanks, Sabe. Somehow I knew you'd be when I first saw you."

As we finished our tea Carrie outlined her plan to me. "You see," she said dreamily, "I still love him . . . and I definitely do not believe in the easy divorce laws we now have. 'What God hath joined together' is still valid to me, and I don't intend for any man—*or* woman—to put that marriage 'asunder' if I can help it."

"I've an idea," I ventured. "It really didn't sound good—in fact it sounded horrible—when the driver told me this morning that all the cabbies in Miami know you. I thought the worst about you for a few minutes."

"This morning? You mean you were planning to leave?" She had a startled look on her face.

"No. He came after me, and I told him I wouldn't go. He was certain I would be handled like the others ahead of me."

She grinned. "That was Jake, of course. And that's good. It will make me appear very unladylike to Mrs. B. She will be pleased to have a report from you, which will protect your sleuthing job for a while longer."

"What did he mean?" I asked. "Do you carry some kind of nameplate so everyone will know you?"

She laughed—hard—then explained.

"My father was a taxi driver in Miami for over fifty years. In fact, he had the first major taxi service in this part of the country after the depression of the thirties, handed down to him from his father, and his grandfather before that when everything was hack or hansom. All the drivers knew him and most of them loved and respected him right up to the time of his death two years ago."

"Well, I couldn't imagine what Jake meant this morning. I was beginning to be suspicious."

"So would Mrs. B. I asked Ron not to tell her anything about me, and I'm sure she hasn't learned much, in spite of her spies. None of the cabbies would talk, that's for sure, and she doesn't know where I work—at least, not so far. She will be horrified to learn of my heritage. She dislikes anyone who serves others."

"That takes in almost the entire world, doesn't it? Owning a fleet of cabs isn't one of the professions, but isn't it as good as producing dresses, no matter how exclusive the shop may be?"

"That is the delightful part of it," Carrie declared. "If she makes things too rough on me, or on Ron, I can always mention—through your reports, of course—that I am thinking of writing my life's story. I can see the tabloid headline now: *Cab Driver's Daughter Secretly Weds Millionaire—Marriage Ends.* When someone tries as hard as Mrs. B, she has to have a few skeletons in her own closet to make her insecure. Yes, I think I have the key to keep her locked up as long as I wish."

"What about Aaron?"

"Ron is the only man for me. Neither of us wanted the divorce, but I was too hurt to fight then . . . and he was intimidated. Now I'm ready to fight. But Ron is going to have to know his own mind and be his own person before we can be happy together. When his mother says 'jump' he will still do it. I believe he must 'leave father and mother and cleave to his wife'—me!"

"One more question. What if she insists that he marry somebody else?"

"Oh, Ron will jump—as he has been trained to do— but he is just stubborn enough to jump backwards or sideways. It will be like my gathering crabs this morning. I always anticipate their being where I don't think they will be."

"That is a real establishment to fight, though, isn't it Carrie? I never could see running down money, but people who establish their own caste systems are really something else."

She was amused. "She thinks I want her money. I'm a nurse. . .I met Ron at the hospital where I work. He'd been in an accident. I didn't know that his mother was a millionaire. I didn't know that his car was a Ferrari—I had heard only that it was totaled and that he was lucky to be alive. During his convalesence I fell in love with a really special person—with wonderful qualities. He fell in love with my terrific back rub."

"He will always love you, Carrie. How could he ever forget your smile?"

Carrie was warm with remembrance. "It was a wonderful marriage, with an interchange of qualities and a capacity for a great deal of growth. . .for the three months it lasted. We complemented each other and had mutual objectives. We were involved in a study group, and he was going to church with me. We were growing together, then his mother entered like a blast of icy wind, and the buds of love withered. I know this sounds a little sticky, but it is how I think of it."

"I understand. No one can really explain in words what his or her own particular type of love is like. I suppose Mrs. B has never forgiven you for taking her boy away?"

"Worse than that. Really, Sabe, she abhors me. She has never seen me or talked to me, yet she hates me. I couldn't offer more money or a prominent name. . . only love."

The discussion was over. It had to be or Carrie would have broken, and I could sense that she would want that least of all right now. For the next hour she tended to the crabs and lunch with a vengeance. I puttered around, trying to brush away the inevitable dust that came from the beach, and whatever else I could do to keep busy.

— — —

Within a month our plans were complete and put into effect. I could understand why Ron had started going to church with Carrie. I found myself kneeling in evening prayer with her every night, and there was such faith in her reliance on God's guidance that I could sense a change in my own life. It was a magnetic force with her. I was surprised at myself, but I began to understand a lot of values I had never thought about before.

I had made regular reports to Mrs. Baker and had learned from her secretary about a homecoming party for Aaron, who had been abroad. Mrs. B had been persistent in her efforts to stimulate interest in Sylvia Newby, whose family was older and better known in the social world than Mrs. B, who was relatively a newcomer.

Carrie planned all the rest of the details through various friends—I didn't know a person could have so many friends—in helpful locations. Then she asked for her vacation time from the hospital.

If Sylvia Newby has trouble getting to the hotel party to welcome Ron back to the States, she can hardly sue all the cab companies for their drivers constantly surrounding her car and delaying her in traffic. Everyone knows that cabbies have their own driving codes. If Carrie happens to be at the hotel, looking radiant in blue velvet, one can hardly blame Ron for remembering the happy marriage he once had and has been missing. If Mrs. B finds her son doesn't jump anymore when she snaps her fingers, it is only the rebellion of youth which most parents experience if they don't allow the person-hood of their children to develop along with growing minds and bodies.

And if I sit oceanside tonight, watching the moon rise over the Atlantic and feeling quite smug about the merits of strategy, I can hardly be expected not to chuckle occasionally over a party crasher and small-time blackmailer who compared notes with a turn-coat spy! Besides, what God has joined together, no mother should ever attempt to put asunder.

Camp
Happening

L ight frost still clung to a few of the low branches, reflecting the brilliance of sunlight through thick pines. The prematurely chill air had just enough snap in it to tint Fern Parker's cheeks a rosy pink, but for once the surrounding beauty failed to fill her with exhilaration.

Woman's intuition, phooey! Fern kicked a rock from the path with the toe of her moccasin as she swung into "Trail No. 3—Craft Barn."

The morning had been wonderful, full of promise and expectancy—the promise of next year's camping season, expectancy of things which might possibly, even probably, happen today.

Fern remembered rolling out before reveille and pulling on a faded corduroy robe.

"Oh, what a beautiful morn-n-ning." The song had come from the icy shower in Bath House No. 5. She rubbed down briskly, brushed her teeth, and bounded up the path again.

"Edie, get up. You're a lazy lout to waste a morning like this. Come alive."

Edith Blackworth, roommate and confidant, groaned

and covered her head. "Go 'way, you wild fern, you!" had come the muffled reply.

How many thousands of years ago had this morning been, Fern wondered as she shuffled along Trail No. 3. For three months she had been an instructor at Springton Youth Camp, and this was the last week of camp. She grimaced as she realized how little time was left with Gary.

The craft barn was at the far end of the camp, at the very foot of Lonesome Mountain. A nature trail led into the wooded area just back of the barn, leading to a high ledge on the mountain. Fern wasn't sure where it had got its name . . . it hadn't been "lonesome" when she and Gary had climbed to the ledge.

Her moccasins hardly made a sound as she entered the barn. The large middle room was empty, and coming in from the bright afternoon sun made the barn seem dark to her and, just for a minute, forbidding.

Near the center of the room was a ladder leading into the loft where Fern felt sure she had left the Fighting Conch and Triton's Trumpet. She remembered showing them to Gary just before his astronomy class yesterday.

"Hello. Come on up," Gary called just over her head. Fern shivered with unexpected delight.

"Hi, Gary. Do you have a class this afternoon?"

"Nope. Just working on this new telescope. I'm planning a little review with it before my final astronomy test Thursday."

Gary's dark head was close to hers as he stooped to help her up the last two rungs. As he smiled at her she could see the little puckers at the corners of his mouth which always appeared when he was especially pleased about something.

Fern's breath came short. Had he any idea at all how handsome he was? How much the kids liked him? He was probably the single most important influence in camp—more than the chaplain, more than the director. He helped kids see what was right and best and urged them to go for that instead of falling short of their abilities.

"I came for my shells," she announced. "Did you find them after I left yesterday?"

"Yes, I meant to tell you last night at campfire. I put them here in the supply desk so they wouldn't get broken. By the way, have you met Nita?"

Fern stood frozen. *Of course* she would be here with Gary. They had been together apparently every minute since she had stopped the sleek Trans-Am in front of the lodge and honked for attention.

Fern managed a noncommittal smile and moved lazily toward the window seat where the girl was sitting.

Be still, heart . . . they'll hear you pounding.

"No, I haven't met Nita," she said, taking in the black-fringed gray eyes, the slightly upturned nose, the auburn hair, and the curved mouth.

"Well, here she is," Gary said. "I've already told her about you."

Here she is, but who is she? Nita Somebody or Nita Nobody? And what have you told her about me, Gary?

Fern decided that whatever it was he had said it had made little impression, because she seemed to feel completely at ease. She was definitely *Nita Somebody* from the way Gary was looking at her. It didn't take the new telescope to discover the effect of a white cardigan topping designer jeans.

"Don't believe a thing Gary tells you." Fern laughed a

small laugh and wondered if it sounded as hollow to them as it did to her. "You really chose a wonderful time to visit camp. They say the last week is always the best."

What a liar I've turned into. It will be the most miserable week of my life!

The sun's rays shining on the window gave Fern a perfect reflection of herself. She wondered why she had ever considered wearing the old plaid shirt which hung loose and made her look boyish. Her blue jeans were thin over the knees. She couldn't see her freckles in the reflection, but she knew they were there—brown dots across her nose, accentuated by the larger brown dots which were her eyes. The very thought made her blush, and she felt the hot blood surge up her tanned throat and into her unruly hair. She ran a dry tongue over drier lips and realized she had forgotten to renew her lipstick.

No wonder Edie calls me a wild fern. My hair is so short and curly it must look like fronds growing in every direction.

How she got away from the barn and spent the remainder of that day she didn't know, but when Edie came back to the cabin just before supper Fern was rolled into a ball under the blankets on her cot. Her eyes were smarting from the tears she refused to release, and her jeans and shirt were in a heap on the floor.

"Fern! What's the matter, kitten?" Edie's husky voice was all sympathy.

"Nothing. Just nothing." Her repeated denial couldn't sound sincere with that catch in her voice.

"Now don't try to fool old Edie. We've been friends too long for that nonsense. Something's wrong, and I want to know about it. We haven't shared every thought for three months to have you suddenly clam up now with that 'Oh, it's nothing' routine."

"Anyway, you know what's wrong, Edie. It's Gary Davis and that Nita Somebody. He didn't say one word about her in three whole months, and every evening since the first week of camp he has spent with me." The words sounded small, but her tight throat was full, and gradually the tears rolled down her cheeks.

"Who's to say he won't be with you tonight, Fern? There's a skate at 7:30." Edie's voice was reassuring, but the question hung heavy in the cabin until the walls seemed to become a sounding board and bounced back the statement, *He won't be with you tonight.* What had Edie said about a skate?

"You'd better hurry up and get dressed if you expect to get to the lodge in time to eat."

"I don't want anything to eat," Fern muttered into her pillow.

"Well, think about it twice," Edie said as she pushed open the cabin door. "Your name is listed on the bulletin board for KP."

The sound of roller skating came through the open windows onto a dimly lighted porch. The music, shouts, and racket of skating were confusing to Fern. She felt a cold night wind blow her hair, and the briskness of it was suddenly relaxing. They would soon be leaving camp, going in different directions. The young people would be going to school. She would be returning to college like most of the other camp leaders. For three months their lives had touched; she felt the better for it, and she hoped those she had worked with would feel the same. She had expected to leave a part of herself here when she left—she had not known it would be her heart.

115

Fern glanced at the two long tables laden with broiled chicken, fish, hamburgers, cheeses of various sorts, and stacks of buns, rye, and pumpernickel for sandwiches. She decided against eating but reached for a paper cup and headed for the hot chocolate table. Soon it would be time for the campers to turn up the lights and devour the food. She wanted to leave before they arrived... healthy youngsters stuffing themselves, sharpening their wits against each other.

"I've been looking for you, Fern. Where have you been all evening?" Gary's voice startled her, and she dropped the cup. With my heart skipping like this I'll never live to be a counselor, she thought wildly as Gary retrieved the cup from under a bench and tossed it into a wire container.

"I wasn't hungry at suppertime," she said, "so I just came up for KP duty afterward."

"I stopped by your cabin before the skate. Edie thought you had gone into town for some exhibit supplies."

"I did start, but on the main road Goldie's left front tire felt low and I thought I'd better wait until morning. That Goldie is always playing tricks on me; one of these days I'm going to surprise her by driving right into a junk yard and leaving her there."

"Poor Goldie," Gary laughed. "Tell me, ma'am, do you always junk your old friends when they get worn out, or when you tire of them?"

His tone was casual, but Fern could detect the underlying question, and she was puzzled by it. Something was wrong here—that should have been her line.

"Only when they refuse to take me places," she evaded.

116

Gary reached for her and drew her closer. "Fern, don't play games with me," he whispered. His fingers pressed into her arm.

Fern looked up at him. "Gary, I'm not clever enough to beat about the bush. What about Nita?"

Gary looked blankly at her. Then he threw back his head and laughed.

"You're jealous! What a wonderful surprise—you're jealous! Nita is my sister."

"Your sister! Oh, no! I've disliked her all day."

"I'm sorry I didn't make it clear, Fern. She always visits during the summer. . . of course, since this is your first year at Springton you couldn't have known that." He chuckled as he leaned down and kissed the tip of her nose.

"Oh, Gary. I want to meet Nita again. I want to see her now as she really is, and not in the unreality of my imagination." Fern started toward the recreation room with a light heart.

"Just a minute, shortie. Meet me halfway?"

By standing on her tiptoes it was easy.

Afternoon Affair

I f someone were to ask Debbie Winters if she still loved her husband after twelve years of marriage, she would answer without hesitation. "I not only love Nick, I am still *in love* with him." This was important to her.

Theirs had been more than a passive love to which she had grown pleasantly accustomed. It stood for the quickened heartbeat she still felt when she heard Nick's steps on the patio and knew he was home again, the sudden glow she sensed when he laughed. But sometimes love didn't seem enough. . . .

Maybe her restlessness came from Nick's being away from home so much. Pilots had schedules to keep which didn't match home plans. Here, then gone for days at a time. Peter and Susan, their fast-growing children, were both in school now, leaving a yawning day from eight to three. Perhaps it was reaching thirty-five and beginning to notice extra lines around her eyes and a need to think about dieting soon. Whatever the reasons, Debbie's days dragged. Time was oddly cumbersome.

Nick's mother always met the children on Fridays after school and kept them for the night. This gave Nick and Debbie an evening to themselves when he was home, and it gave Debbie time to shop when he wasn't. That is how Debbie met Bruce Harris one warm afternoon during late September. She had driven into town to shop, though she didn't really need anything. Then she went to a much-publicized movie, which wasn't good enough to hold her interest. Halfway through it she walked out. The plot and dialogue were indecent, the actors unbelievably crass.

"Debbie! How in the world are you? You're as beautiful as ever."

It was a familiar voice, but for a minute she could not place it, even as she looked at its owner. He was a large man with dark hair beginning to gray a bit. Then his smiling gray eyes gave him identity.

"Why Bruce, when did you come back to this area? I haven't seen you for years." It seemed impossible that she could have forgotten him. He had been her first love, years ago in high school.

"Things are great, Debbie. Just great."

"How's Linda? Any children yet?"

"Linda and I split up about five years ago. Fortunately there were no children." It was a moment which might have been embarrassing, but Bruce's smile kept it from being so. "She's remarried now." He looked very right with his world.

"So, tell me all the news. Are you living here, or just visiting?"

"I was transferred back here by my engineering firm. I should have called you and Nick, but you know how it is. I've been busy getting the feel of the city again for about three months now . . . say, do you have time for a cup of coffee?"

"I'd love a cup of coffee." Debbie was glad to see this

old friend, the man she undoubtedly would have married if she had not met Nick at college.

Bruce guided her into a small cafe. He was relaxed, unhurried, assured of what to do with his extra time.

Reacquaintance began easily, naturally. They had a lot of friends in common. "Remember Tricia? She married Chuck after all those years. Almost like marrying her brother, I'd think. . .but they seem happy."

"What's happened to Jack? Ever get over his drinking problem?"

"Hadn't you heard? He was killed in an accident two years ago. Drunken driving."

Debbie was eager to talk about Nick, their children, their new home in the suburbs, their old dog. . .but somehow Bruce was always quick with a question, a comment, which left her immediate life out of the conversation.

It was nice to get together. And because Nick and the children were not at home, the cup of coffee lasted past dinner and a drive "to see how the city had changed."

— — —

November's Indian summer camped on the hills a long time, misting the nights and leaving the days golden and hazy. Every Friday afternon since they had met accidentally, Bruce was somehow available in spite of his engineering duties. He would suggest movies, or a drive, or just a long afternoon walk. It was incredible, but it happened that every time Nick was away, Bruce called.

"Have I missed that fella again, Debbie?"

"He was called to fill in for one of the other pilots."

Once in a while Bruce dropped by her home. There was some matter needing attention not too far from her

120

house. He was just in the area. Once or twice he dropped in during the evening on the off-chance that he might catch Nick at home.

They had always enjoyed bantering with each other, and importantly, he did not press their friendship. He did not try to romance her, so it did not really seem strange to be meeting each week, to be reserving thoughts and anecdotes for Bruce. Certainly not strange at all, until one beautiful day . . . when Nick's plane was hijacked.

They heard it on the car radio as they drove out to play miniature golf in the late fall sunshine.

"Captain Nick Winters, a fifteen-year veteran pilot, reported by radio that the hijacker is a woman, apparently adept with knives. Captain Winters reported that both stewardesses are being held hostage and their lives threatened unless the flight continues to Cuba. So far there has been no demand for money. It is assumed the hijacking is for political reasons. There is some speculation as to whether or not there will be enough fuel, however; flight authorities are hopeful that Captain Winters will be able to land the plane safely. Important passengers on this flight include a well-known lyric soprano. . . . "

Debbie snapped off the newscast. Methodically, one by one, she began to think of their years together. Dear Nick. Friend Nick. Husband Nick. Lover Nick. Father Nick. Nick, whose deep laughter made her heart sing.

Bruce was looking at her curiously. His eyes were veiled, his lips tightly set. He offered no word of encouragement or even sympathy. As she looked at him she knew that he had been playing for time, gaining her trust. . . . It didn't matter. Nothing would ever really

121

matter again except her family. Nick, her children, Nick's mother, and even their old dog. God had been so good to her, so patient. . . .

"I want to go home, Bruce."

He turned the car slowly. For a long while he didn't say anything as he drove along the quiet streets.

"I guess I've lost you again, Debbie. It will always be Nick, won't it?"

How could it be otherwise? How could he have thought she was his to lose again?

"I must be there, waiting. He will call me as soon as he can. I must be home," she said.

Debbie knew she should say something clever, or perhaps something completely honest. She could only say, "Hurry please. I *must* be home when he calls."

Homecoming

The last bar of sunlight slanted through the great library windows of the university as Marta O'Brian entered. Mrs. Pierce, known as "The Iron Fence" among the daytime students, was reluctantly relinquishing her seat of honor to less strict and better-liked Miss Paxton.

Purposely Marta selected a table near the end of the room. She felt that here she could study without interference from "the gang" as they made their way in and out of the library to look over the situation and see if anyone of football importance might be studying. It was simply amazing how many girls suddenly remembered exams they must cram for when football personalities occupied the library.

A single book lay on the table Marta selected. She opened her own notebook and began to review her outline on literature. In the middle of the Greek classics the person belonging to the book across the table brought an armful of other books to keep it company and quietly scraped back the chair. Even before glancing up Marta felt her heart skip a beat as she realized it was Jimmy Koyle. She smiled and gathered her papers closer to her to give him room to spread out the volumes he carried.

Jimmy was one of those campus men all the girls sighed over, without hope of ever attracting his attention. He was a premed student and, like most students who knew they had a number of hard years before them, seemed to give his full attention to his work. After one quick grin at Marta he was lost in his studies.

Marta watched him study. His red hair was a bright contrast to dark brown eyes. . . and he had the most sensitive looking hands she had ever seen. Obviously he was as unconquerable as the Greek gods Marta was supposed to be studying about. . . .

When at last her review was completed she was pleased to see Jimmy piling up his books to return to Miss Paxton. He slipped her a note, and Marta felt her face brighten like a neon light. Who wouldn't want Jimmy to walk to the dorm with her? And how like a future doctor he was, protective already. His note read: "You look tired. Since you have a big day ahead of you, you should go to bed early. I'll walk to the dorm with you." Marta forgot about the two errands she had intended to do after leaving the library. They could wait. Here was an opportunity not to be missed, and besides Jimmy hadn't asked a question—he had made a statement.

It was a beautiful October night. The harvest moon hung low over the treetops, and everything shimmered in its golden haze.

"You're quite a girl to be selected by the football team as queen," Jimmy began the conversation. "You were my choice, too."

"How nice of you to tell me," Marta responded. "I really thought Eileen or Patty would get the votes, but I can't deny I'm happy about winning."

"Of course you're glad. That's human nature. But the other girls didn't stand a chance. Eileen is pretty—probably prettier than any other girl on campus—but she isn't friendly. And Patty is pretty, too, but she looks as if she's been chiseled from stone. There's no heart . . . no inner fire."

"You can really disect a person! But don't stop now, Jimmy. I want your description of me. Those of Eileen and Patty were completely right, now that I think of it, but I'm not so easy. I don't think I'm especially pretty." She waited impatiently for Jimmy's answer as she matched her stride to his.

At last he chuckled. "You *are* a little more difficult to describe," he said. "In fact, I don't think I will, but I'll tell you why you'll be queen tomorrow. Because you're a pixy . . . a pixy with a purpose."

Marta laughed at this unexpected answer. "Now—will you describe a pixy for me?" she asked. "And what is my purpose?"

"Later," was his singular reply as they came to the foot of the dorm steps.

The shadows of the trees lingered here and Marta caught her breath as Jimmy stepped close to her. The well-memorized speech she had repeated so often since her first dating days sprang to her tongue, but the words were not uttered. Jimmy touched the tiny dimple in her chin with one finger and said, "Bye." Then he was off down the walk with his long strides and a tuneless whistle. As she walked into the dorm she realized that she very much had wanted Jimmy to be attracted to her. She had purposely talked about herself and had not had the courtesy to ask about his interests; then, as a last rudeness, she hadn't had the presence of mind to thank him for walking with her.

"Football queen!" she muttered to herself as she entered her room. "*Flub* queen!"

— — —

Homecoming at the university was a full weekend of activities crowded together and trampled down by people. Marta was crowned by the team's captain and presented an armful of roses by Rear Admiral Leath who once had attended the college. She was in a whirl the entire time. The crown set upon her glossy "fro" gave her the look of a mischievous elf trying hard to have the dignity to rule her subjects.

"Play for Marta—play for your queen," chanted the crowd led by the cheerleaders as the game progressed. The roar which rose at the final score—37 to 36—was deafening. "Rah, rah—team! Rah, rah—queen!"

Only once during the weekend did Marta see Jimmy. Her escort for the events was, of course, the football captain, much to his usual date's chagrin. Just as he placed the crown upon her head, Marta glanced into the sea of faces before her and for a fleeting moment, saw Jimmy's red hair. He smiled at her . . . and then came the ceremonies, game, and get-togethers which carried her through the balance of homecoming surrounded by a host of friends, both old and newly acquired.

Following Sunday vespers the campus was suddenly quiet. The last good-byes had been said; the last visitors had left with a flurry of waving hands.

Restless after the bustle and confusion, Marta left the dorm for a walk. She hoped it would help counter the letdown which always followed such high tension.

The broad walks of the campus fell behind her. The

126

gravel road beside the conservatory, vacant on Sunday evenings, stretched before her in what could well represent a single path with no turning.

"Now, after such a grand weekend," Marta murmured to herself, "why should I feel lonely?"

A crunch on the gravel behind her caused her to give a startled look over her shoulder. Quickly closing the gap between them was Jimmy. She stopped and waved to him.

"Your roommate said that you were walking alone and that this is your favorite route," he announced with his usual directness.

"I am, and it is . . . but I'm glad you caught up with me," she replied. Marta was anxious to know why Jimmy had looked for her, but she was determined this time not to talk about herself.

He noticed her quizzical look and grinned down at her. "Hi, pixy," he said.

"Of course I can't resist asking you again for your definition of *that* word."

"A pixy," he explained as they turned again toward the campus, "is mischievous, interesting, and always happy. You're a combination of all three."

"I remember you said the other night that I had a purpose too—what does that mean?"

"It means that although you are full of fun, and make life interesting for those around you, and manage to stay sweet and happy all at the same time—I know that you do these things with purpose. It is a part of your life's philosophy, or perhaps your religion. When I found out how 'tuned in' you are to Christian principles I started reading your church literature and found the secret, I

think. 'Man is that he might have joy'...sound familiar?"

"Why Jimmy—you make me feel I have a lot to live
up to. Yes, it does sound familiar, and yes, I *do* try to be
that type of person. I admit I much prefer your adjectives to any others you might have used to describe
me—but I can hardly believe you have read my church
literature."

"That's only because I admire your attitude. For in-
stance, you were really great during homecoming. Some
girls would have acted differently to try to get the honor
in the first place. And some would low-key their religious convictions in an effort to be more popular. I'm
impressed that you carried your whole person with you
to the top."

"Well, you embarrass me a little, because I don't
carry my whole person as stoutly as I'd like, but thanks
for noticing me. I had a really busy weekend, and I
wanted to be me." Marta was serious, but her eyes
crinkled with pleasure because here she was with one of
the "most wanted" men on campus delving into her
psyche. "I saw you only once."

"Every time I saw you, you were surrounded by a
crowd. When I went to your dorm a while ago it was to
see if the queen would take a walk with me, but I'm glad
you were already walking. I'm a little shy around girls."

Marta was truly a pixy (with a purpose) when she
laughed. "I doubt if you're shy after you're with a girl,
Jimmy. You don't seem so at all. It's probably just thinking about it that bothers you. At least, that's how my
brother Joe is."

"Right as usual," he answered.

The glow of the dorm windows loomed up before

them. A light mist had begun to fall, and the harvest moon of last night had dissipated. Jimmy clasped Marta's hand as they hurried to the door.

"Bye again," he said. "May I see you soon. . .for a movie or something?"

"Of course, Jimmy," she answered. "Whenever your studies are finished I'll be waiting."

Marta climbed the stairs to her room. It's funny, she mused, how two days ago I thought of homecoming as a group of noisy, fun-loving people, and it worried me a lot how to be myself and still play the role of "queen" I had been elected to fill. Now it seems like a time just for Jimmy and me—coming through a dark mist into brightness—coming home.

Come
Back
for
Thanksgiving

There was something compelling about Mike's invitation which I felt helpless to ignore. It was something special drawing me to his home which had nothing to do with the holiday or with our tragedy which had occurred there. Rather it was a feeling of expectancy.

For a week I argued with myself, reviewing the reasons I should not take my children to visit their Uncle Mike. I had turned down my brother-in-law's invitations time and again during the last three years. Now the children were getting old enough to insist that we go.

"Come back for Thanksgiving, Doreen," he said once more. In the end I gave in, as I had suspected from the beginning I would. The fact was I also wanted to go back—I could think of little else.

When I telephoned my sister to tell her of my decision there was such complete silence I thought for a moment the phone had gone dead.

"Are you still there?"

"Yes, I'm here, Doreen."

"Well, I wanted you to know where we'd be in case you called and couldn't reach us." She had planned, I knew, to ask us to her home for the holiday. I had declined before she had gotten around to asking.

"I just wish you would stay away from that place, especially this time of year," my sister got in the last word. "Anywhere would be better than there... *anywhere!*"

The trip on Wednesday passed quickly. Tom, who would be fourteen soon, took charge of Nan and Don. The twins, at ten, could be easily entertained when their older brother bent his will to it. Tom, Jr., was so much like his father—completely charming—when he played with them. My husband had always kept our children occupied when he was alive.

As the miles flew by I reminisced about the home my sister had referred to as "that place."

The lovely old farmhouse was full of sunshine by day and friendly squeaks by night, leaning into the wind off the river. There were wide doors and tall windows, huge stone hearths in most of the rooms, and informally planted gardens around the clapboard and stone exterior. Rambling along the acreage closest to the house were loose stone walls hugging the earth from which they had come, yet high enough to discourage horses from wandering too close to the gardens. In back of the pastures was a dense wood where Mike and Tom and I used to tramp around. There had always been the three of us—Mike and his brother Tom, and the scrawny adolescent I had been while growing up in the tenant farmhouse a mile down the road.

Of course the house and land had become Mike's—he was the older brother. But the woods belonged to all of us, as unencumbered of ownership as the stars. So it seemed to us. Those were the woods where Tom had asked me to marry him—and where ten years later a trespassing hunter searching for quail or pheasant had made a wild shot . . . and Tom lay dead. That was nearly four years ago, but my sister still worried about my visiting the farm. She thought it would stir up only bad memories which I could avoid if I would just keep away from "that place."

I had tried to explain. "That friendly old house where Tom lived as a boy would bring far more happy memories than sad ones."

"Nonsense. You are remembering your happy youth."

"Quite right, of course. I remember the eager young girl I was once. I believe I could also walk through the damp woods and feel close to Tom . . . and somehow content." My sister was not an outdoor person. She had never heard the wind whisper to her or read the essays the sunshine wrote upon the leaves.

"Can't you accept Tom's death? He's a memory now. That's all."

"How can you be so sure he is nothing? Who gave you an insight into death?" I always became angry at this point. "Besides," I would rationalize because I was not at all certain she wasn't right, "I think it would be good for the children to explore the woods, as I did, finding its quiet, peaceful places."

My sister never stopped short of the last word. "Just be sure your own life goes on, Doreen. You're too obsessed with what *was*, not what *is*." To her it was simple. Every issue in life was either black or white. There was never gray for her. . . .

Mike was waiting for us when we drove up the long lane to the house. He rushed down the steps to shake hands with Tom, Jr., and to swing the twins around before they bounded up onto the wide porch, full of re-membering. His clear blue eyes were kind and friendly as they matched his smile of welcome to me. He gave no hint of our last evening together when he had asked me to marry him and let him help fill the void his brother had left in the children's lives, and in mine. I knew he was too proud to repeat the proposal.

"You've stayed away too long," he said simply.

I sniffed the sharp wind off the river and glanced at the overcast sky. Our breath was frosting in the air as we talked. "How wrong my sister has been, Mike. I feel alive again for the first time since we left here."

"We all have hang-ups of one kind or another. Your sister tries to saddle you with some of hers."

"Not really—at least, not consciously. She tries to help, but she doesn't understand."

He circled my shoulders companionably with a broad arm and led me up the steps while directing the children about the luggage.

"The twins packed for themselves. I'm afraid they have brought enough to last a month."

"I wish they were staying a month." He might have said more, but I was grateful that he hadn't.

"Uncle Mike," Nan shrilled joyously. "We have a whole extra day out of school."

"Yes, but our teacher gave us extra assignments, too." Don was always pessimistic about homework.

Indoors the old house still creaked in its joints as brightly burning logs in the fireplace cast reflections into dark corners of the room. The twins began jumping around their uncle again, and Tom, Jr., was trying to outshout them with information about his science project. I felt a pang of conscience at having kept the children away from Mike so much. The only times they had seen him after we had left the farm had been when he came to the city and stayed over for dinner with us in our apartment. Mike needed the country. He was that kind of man, as Tom had been. Apparently the children needed the country too.

"The woods is calling me, Mike." The words tumbled from my lips unexpectedly. "Is it too late for a walk?"

"Yes." He was curt. "We'll all go tomorrow."

He stopped his play with the children and sent them on a trek to the kitchen for milk and cookies before he explained. "I've sold most of the woods, Doreen."

I must have looked shocked, or perhaps hurt, for he hastened on, though his words were carefully selected. "The land is needed for development, and I have more than I need or want." He went on, but I ceased to listen. I felt that a part of me had been hacked and felled and carted off.

"I don't allow any hunting in the woods these days," I heard him saying.

"Can't you. . ." I began, and stopped to moisten my lips with a dry tongue. "Can't you just post 'no hunting' signs?"

"I've tried, but some people refuse to read signs. I have deeded some of the land across the river to the state for a wildlife preserve. In a few months there will only be five acres of timber behind the cleared acreage here on this side—a spot to retreat to once in a while, but not large enough to attract a lot of hunters anymore."

Mike was going into great detail, and I heard him talking on and on. Once in a while I heard a strange, tight voice which I knew to be my own asking questions, making comments which probably made little sense. In-

134

side me a trembling voice kept repeating *Nowhere...*
nowhere to come home to!

I slept little that night and arose earlier than the
others. The morning was crisp and still, with early light
filtering dimly through cumulus clouds—a day of
thanks. After dressing hurriedly, I slipped out of the
house and made my way through dew-soaked grasses to
the edge of the woods. I supposed I should have waited
for Mike and the children, as he had suggested, but I
couldn't make a "formal" visit to these woods I knew as
well as my own living room.

A startled deer stopped grazing, poised to dart into
the security of the thicket. Patiently I waited until he
resumed his eating before I followed one of the nature
trails into the dampness of the wood. Here early sunlight
dappled only the bark of the trees, for most of the leaves
still clung tenaciously to the life already flowing from
them, waiting for frost.

Thanksgiving Day again—four years since Tom had
entered these same woods in search of peace and had
found death instead. Somehow I had sensed then that
the woods, too, must pass away. Perhaps this was why
Mike had insisted we visit the farm again this year. He
had known that I must be made to face reality in many
ways *sometime, somewhere.* He had shown me the time,
allowed me the where before the destruction of bull-
dozers.

A covey of quail startled up beside me, the sudden
whirring of their wings raising the gooseflesh on me.
"How utterly beautiful," I whispered as they scattered.
"How free and wild."

I do not remember seeing the flash or hearing the gun,
but several pellets tore into my flesh. I was frightened to

move for fear the wounds were deeper than I knew. I should have cried out—the hunter could not have been far away and might have helped me—but I crouched silently, waiting for death to come to me as it had come to my husband. There is no way of remembering how long it was before I realized I was still breathing.

"I have things to do. I don't want to die yet," I heard myself saying. Perhaps time trembles, or hesitates, in emergencies. I became aware that my head felt heavy and the wounds in my chest were bleeding considerably. Strange, the thoughts that went through my brain—how the blood would ruin the green suede which Tom had given me, but of course it was worn out anyway; how friendly were the sighs and creaks of the old house last night (was it only hours ago?); how there seemed always to have been Mike and Tom and me, and now there were only Mike and me and Tom's children.

Tom seemed very close there in the woods; I felt his nearness. If I closed my eyes I would see him, showing me the trail he had taken.

I heard myself talking to him. "You are. You still live, even though it is in another place now. I'm glad, Tom. I'm so glad to believe you still exist, as Mike told me you did live somewhere! It's your religion, Tom—it is the faith that you and Mike always had, even as children, which first made you so valuable to me as persons. Oh, Tom, I have not taught our children what you wanted— to have faith in this life and the life to come, but I will, Tom. I promise I will—because in my heart I have known it was right all along. So I can't, you see. . . I can't close my eyes and come with you now. It would be so easy to do that, but I mustn't—not now. Your children are here, and they need me to teach them. Would

Mike do it for me? Yes, but Mike needs me too. I could not see this yesterday, Tom. Not before today. I wanted only you, and I would not release the tight holding of my love for you. Now I know I have love for you forever in my heart, and enough love for Mike too."

I remembered my sister's saying *anywhere* was better than this farm, and I wondered if she would consider death better. Then I felt my own *nowhere* to belong, and knew I belonged here—Mike's belief in the *somewhere* beyond this life, and Tom's existence in that *otherwhere* which I could feel but not quite see. They seemed to all run together, these thoughts of mystery, but I must not close my eyes to see them better, fused into one place. I must keep my eyes wide open so I wouldn't pass out.

They must find me . . . I must not sleep. . . .

Then, on a wave of red fog I heard Mike. O God, thank you. I hear Mike calling me. Your brother is coming, Tom. He will not let me go with you now. . . . Your children will know your home, Tom, and your faith in God. And I will not yet know your otherwhere!

Then I began to scream so Mike could find me. It was a good loud noise, and it sounded wonderful coming from my throat, forced from healthy lungs. As long as I could make a sound like that I would be all right. I screamed, and screamed, and screamed. . . .

The
Clairvoyant

Almost above us the uninterrupted traffic of the freeway swished along at breakneck speed. "When I hear that roar of motors above us," I confided to Marcia, "I'm not sure it was such a good idea to come down here just to have our fortunes told, especially when we don't believe in the occult in the first place."

"There are plenty of places more convenient to reach and certainly more conducive to our peace of mind where we could hear the same sort of fantasy," she answered.

"Curiosity, I suppose." I laughed at our doing such a thing. "Atmosphere. We needn't have come down here just because Helena saw the sign . . . but we had to investigate."

"She knew we would. That's what comes of driving around on a Saturday instead of putting ourselves to work doing something worthwhile." Marcia grimaced, feeling a bit of guilt, I suppose, as I was feeling.

"My fortune hasn't been told since I was a teenager at a county fair."

"What were you told," Marcia asked sarcastically, "that you would be a schoolteacher?" She was always negative, always grumpy, and enjoyed it immensely.

"Do you know I can't remember a word that she said? I *do* remember what my parents said when they knew I had gone there. They quoted scripture and told me to keep away from anything that was not 'of good report'!"

I parked the car and Helena hurried ahead to pound on the door of the dilapidated house where a rusted knocker hung under faded signs of the Zodiac. The building squatted in the flats of an old riverbed far beneath the ridge on which the freeway had been built. A small creek still meandered along the ravine. Had the spot been landscaped, or even left to nature, it might have been quite lovely. As it was, old tires, rusting cans, and other debris had been dumped at one time or another into the former riverbed. A narrow side road which led onto the flats from the ridge above was nearly obscured by weeds. The ruts once made by cars and rain had begun to fill in. The footpath leading to the house was matted with dead weeds.

As we stood at the door we could hear someone muttering inside. "That can't be Marcia muttering," Helena teased. "She's out here with us."

We were hardly prepared for the old woman who eventually stood framed in the doorway. Her skin was more dirty than dark-complexioned, and the colors of the clothing she wore had long since faded into gray. She stood staring at us, from one to the other, but mostly at me. She frowned and passed a hand before her eyes as though she were trying to erase something. I noticed her stained and broken fingernails.

At last she smiled, exposing decayed teeth, and beckoned Helena and Marcia to follow her inside. Although she turned her back on me, I followed the others.

None of us believed this old woman had the power to foresee the future any more than we ourselves could be sensitive to the times, the format of the world powers, the interaction of human lives. We just thought it would be more fun to make-believe than to openly disbelieve whatever she would have to tell us. As we followed her into the dimly lit house, however, I felt a wave of apprehension that raised gooseflesh. Parental instructions of years ago came to mind, and I knew I was where I should not be. "If you would not want Christ to walk beside you into a place," my father had said, "you should not go there."

"Tea leaves or palm reading?" she queried, her deep-set eyes glaring at me from beneath a craggy brow. She had a red kerchief wrapped around her wispy hair, giving an illusion of glowing embers on whitened ash. I found myself wondering if she were really as old as she looked—if indeed it would be possible for a person to be so old and still alive.

"Palm reading for all of us," I blurted out loudly in the silence. She had not directed her question to me, but I had not given the others a chance to decide. My stomach had already done a few flips before settling into a rolling pattern of partial nausea. The heavy odors of stale food permeated the ramshackle place, and the scurrying of roaches along the baseboards convinced me that the drinking of tea was out of the question. I had never seen cockroaches on the move like this, oblivious to daylight and the presence of human beings.

Helena, always eager to rush into any situation, volunteered to be the first to follow the old woman into an inner room. Marcia and I strained to hear what was being said. One look at Helena's face as she rejoined us led to further misgivings.

"What did she tell you?" Marcia demanded.

"Not a thing," Helena answered. "She just told me I didn't believe in fortune telling and I had no business wasting her time."

Marcia insisted on being next. "I'm not going to wait until last," she said "or I won't have the strength to get out of here. My knees are shaking already. This place is *spooky!*" Her grumbling came back to us as she stalked down the hall toward the fortune teller.

"Well?" I said to Helena when we were alone.

"Nothing," she whispered. "She told me absolutely nothing."

We discussed that as we waited. Each time I ventured to laugh about our "adventure" and seek some word from her she avoided my eyes.

"What's the matter?" I said at length. "If she didn't tell you anything why are you upset—which I definitely think you are?" It seemed to me that she was being obstinate. Or silly. Or afraid.

It seemed an interminably long time before Marcia returned. Like Helena, she refused to look at me when she entered the room. She pulled her collar up around her throat, hunched up her shoulders into a shrug beneath the wild plaid of her coat, and jerked her head toward the inner room.

"Your turn," she said.

"Is it worth it?"

"Maybe for you. Go find out for yourself," she answered shortly.

Inside, seated on a straight chair across from the old woman, I was startled to have her stare at me with contempt. My gaze fell on a Bible under her hand, and I am sure my eyes blazed at her. It seemed ludicrous as well as blasphemous to connect palm reading with the Bible.

"I would tell them nothing, do you understand? Nothing," she screeched before I could comment on the Bible.

Now for the first time I felt anger—anger that we had wasted our time and money on this old woman. Mostly I felt anger at myself because this person could look at me and make shivers run down my spine.

"The first one," she went on, "she begs to hear. She says she believes, but I know she does not. The other openly says she does not believe, that I am a hoax. 'Why does she say she does not believe?' I ask myself. Then I know. It is *your* fault!" she shouted at me. "I knew it when I saw you standing at my door."

"My fault? For what—their not believing in your claim to see the future?"

"No, no. It is your fault that you have come to my door today. It is in your eyes that you bring ill tidings for me. Your eyes are not a color—they change and change—first blue, then green, then yellow brown. It is an omen! I fear you, I *hate* you!"

I stood up, feeling an impulse to run. I had never had a person tell me I was hated before. "Well, I'm sorry that my eyes are hazel, and I know they do change. They always have. But you need not fear me or hate me. I can't help it, you know, and I wouldn't do a thing to cause you harm."

For a moment she glared at me without saying more. Then she motioned for me to sit again. In a hoarse whisper she began to tell of bad omens for the day, which she seemed to think would affect her instead of me.

"*You* are the leader," she accused, and I strangely felt that she was telling her own fortune, not mine. I remembered that Helena had first seen the sign on the secondary road telling of the fortune teller. It was Marcia who had complained that there wasn't anywhere worth going right now anyway so we might as well indulge Helena this side trip. Maybe my driving the car could be interpreted as "leading" us here.

"You knew I had no fortune for either of those others," she wheezed, leaning toward me. "Not even for you. There is no future. All I see is disaster, chaos. You are destroying me . . . today!"

"Come on, now," I began to reason with her. "Surely you don't go on like this for everyone who stops here for a reading." I tried to smile and thought she might let up on the dramatics a bit. "This was just a 'fun day' for us. We don't know you, and you are quite right—we do not believe in the occult in any way—but that shouldn't bother you. Isn't it the money you want? Do *you* believe in yourself?"

A once-ornate curtain separated this room from the hall we had traveled to reach it. Glancing toward it, I could see Marcia and Helena peeking past the hanging, wide-eyed and supposedly afraid.

"I don't know," she answered. The tears began to brim over her red-rimmed eyes and course along the wrinkles of her cheeks. I glanced at the others for reassurance, but got none.

Then she began once more to screech at me about her future which would be changed from this day, and about my eyes which changed color. The ranting grew

143

in intensity until I began to fear her. She might be insane, living out here alone. I knew she was too weak and old to harm us, but the fear persisted. I stood up again, and found myself trembling. My mind caught savagely at the scriptures which advised staying away from strange or evil spirits and adhering to righteousness. Then I turned and ran from the room. Helena and Marcia followed after me.

"Sensitivity I can understand," I panted as all three of us ran out the front door. "A person's being phychic I can accept...but this woman is out of my element."

The rasping voice still shouted at us as we hurried down the tangled path to the car. Marcia began grumbling again. "Whose brilliant idea was this, anyway? That old witch is paranoid. Whatever happened to the 'tall, dark, and handsome' routine?"

"She gave me the creeps," Helena affirmed with a shaky voice. "I mean, she really did. I almost believed her."

Marcia and I exchanged knowing glances. Gullible Helena would swallow almost anything. "She must have believed it herself, or she wouldn't have repeated it so often."

"It was halfway convincing," I admitted. "I think she should not live out here all alone. She probably *is* a bit crazy."

At Helena's expression I continued. "On the other hand, maybe this is all part of an act. Maybe she thinks it will bring her more business if she makes a sensational impression."

"Well, *I'm* impressed." Helena's eyes were as big as a child's after hearing a ghost story.

We had to laugh. Outside in the sunshine the whole

thing began to be a joke to us. "All the same," Marcia admonished, "we ought to keep away from that sort of thing."

Our fears were leaving us. Even Helena was giggling as our compact car began to nose up the twisting incline toward the secondary road.

"I don't believe that stuff fortune tellers dream up," Helena began bravely, "any more than you do. But you must admit that she had a certain flair. . . ."

Her words were choked off as we saw a huge truck before us, attempting to turn onto the track we had just struggled through. A man hailed us, demanding that we stop, and two more men with machetes walked toward the car. "They're. . . they're not going to go down there and hurt her, are they?" Helena gasped.

"Her? What about us?" Marcia had turned white.

I rolled down my window a crack. "What's the trouble?" I asked, securing the lock and checking our possible passage around them. Then I noticed the county seal on the side of the truck. One of the men sauntered closer to the car.

"This property is going to be landscaped," he said. "Notice was given over six weeks ago that all habitation must cease. You the only ones living here?"

"We don't live here," Marcia sputtered. "What do you take us for?"

"My friends and I just saw a sign about the fortune-teller who lives down there," I explained.

"That old woman still there?" one of the men asked. "I thought she'd be gone now—she was told over six weeks ago that we'd be here today."

"I'll report it on the radio," the leader said. "She knows that this isn't her property and that it has been designated as a park. The shack she lives in was condemned years ago. We've told her a dozen times, at least, that she'd have to move."

"Maybe she hasn't anywhere to go," Helena suggested.

"Ma'am," the man replied, "her bank account has been checked by the authorities. She could buy out all of us."

"The trees are to be left," the foreman called to the workers, turning away from the car. "The rest of us will start on this brush. Take care of that fortune-teller sign up there," he called to another.

Beneath us the house was silhouetted against the riverbed. Tangled sumac, ragweed, and prairie grass, choking around it would be hacked out and replaced with manicured plantings. I wondered where the old woman would go—what hole she would find to burrow into. Or would she clean herself up and use her money to live comfortably in her last years? I supposed I could be interpreted as the leader of today's trouble for her....I had driven into her road just before the truck which would destroy her home. Even though she knew, she had not accepted that. She had somehow blamed me.

Cautiously we traveled down the secondary road to the freeway. For an instant I closed my hazel eyes. Across a visionary baseboard ran a deserting army of roaches.

Skin
Deep

This morning I was shopping for Christmas gifts and, like most early shoppers, I was more or less looking things over before making decisions. I'm rather impulsive when I shop for gifts—I purchase what seems to reach out and grab me as I walk past. Invariably the gift suits the person I had in mind as I picked it up, so I have learned through the years to wait for this special feeling as I pass by an object. Today, however, a distractingly loud voice disrupted my tour up and down aisles.

"Are you sure this is what you want? I don't know what you can be thinking."

"Yes ma'am," came a lower voice in reply. "This is what I want."

"Well, you'd better look around some more. Maybe you'll find something you like better, something more . . . personal. You don't have to rush."

"I like this fine, Mrs. Van." The voice was low but definite.

"You simply must look around some more, Rosemary. That's only twenty dollars, and I've told you I'm willing to pay as much as twenty-five this year."

The conversation was distinguishable from two aisles

away, but as I sauntered closer the context of it became clearer. In fact, I recognized the louder voice. Its owner and I had worked together on various PTA and civic projects in our neighborhood.

"Mrs. Vanhouser. It's nice to see you again," I said as I walked alongside "the voice."

"Oh, hello." She gave me a disinterested look of recognition. Then, adjusting to my interruption of her discourse, she turned toward me with an attitude of consternation.

"I'm trying to get my Christmas shopping done early because Mr. Van and I are going out of town for the holidays. Rosemary, here, is insisting on my buying a stuffed animal for her Christmas gift. Have you ever heard of such a thing? A stuffed animal for a grown woman!"

Rosemary, obviously embarrassed by the loudness of her employer's conversation nevertheless knew what she wanted. Her chin jutted forward with determination.

"Hello, Rosemary." I ignored the complaint and the lack of introduction. "My name is Rose too."

She looked at me questioningly, then quietly said, "Hello."

Rosemary was a tall woman, with large hands and feet, solidly poised now against the onslaughts of "the voice." In her arms she held a purple poodle with a bright green bow tied about the neck. She stroked the nose, pushing plush against the grain, then smoothing it down again.

"I think her selection is unquestionably the best of the lot. If she has chosen what she wants, what is the problem?" I asked casually, realizing that I was interrupting a discussion between employer and maid, but

148

instinctively wanting to defend Rosemary. This was not so much because of her position as a maid but because she had been encouraged to make a choice, then had the wisdom of it questioned. Why bring her to the store to make a selection and then criticize it?

In my mind there were a number of reasons why Rosemary had chosen the purple poodle. If she had a child in her life who would be delighted at the wonderful surprise of a large stuffed animal on Christmas morning, why select something for herself that she didn't need or want? I resisted saying all the clever and sarcastic things that came to mind and even managed a small smile for "the voice."

"Well, one problem is that I have set aside twenty-five dollars for Rosemary's gift, and this toy is only twenty."

I could hardly keep from laughing at Mrs. Vanhouser's petulent expression because things were not going as she had planned. Then, putting on a mask of concern, I said, "At Christmastime who counts the cost of a gift if it pleases the recipient? You could always buy some fruit or nuts or cheese to make up the difference. Food is a big item these days, and I think it makes a lovely gift."

"Perhaps you're right," she agreed. "And I'm running out of time anyway." She turned again to the quiet woman beside her, "Are you really *sure* this is what you want?"

"Yes, ma'am." Rosemary confirmed her choice once more. "I like it real well."

Her wide lips smiled at me now, and the corners of her eyes crinkled. We understood each other.

After Mrs. Vanhouser and Rosemary left I stood looking at the stuffed toys. Suddenly one seemed to reach out and grab me. I picked it up and began stroking the gray and brown plush against the grain, then smoothing it down again. Could I really do what I had in mind?

"How much is this?" I asked the clerk.

"The talking ones are all twenty-five dollars," she replied.

I found the ring and pulled. The sound was exactly what I wanted—I would just have to scrimp on something else to make up for the purchase.

"I want this one wrapped and delivered." I scribbled the address and handed it to the clerk. "Please be certain to enclose this note from me: *To show you how nice it is to receive a stuffed animal at Christmas!*" Then I headed back to my parked car to make peace with myself.

When Mrs. Vanhouser passes her unexpected gift on, as I am sure she will, I sincerely hope it will appear to Rosemary to be a docile little Christmas donkey rather than the braying jackass I sent to her employer.